GAME CHANGER

KING OF THE COURT #1

PIPER LAWSON

Copyright © 2023 Piper Lawson Books

All Rights Reserved.

No part or parts of this publication may be reproduced, stored in a retrieval system, or transmitted in any form or by any means, electronic, mechanical, photocopying, recording, or otherwise, in any language, without the prior written permission of the copyright owner.

This book is sold subject to the condition that it shall not, by way of trade or otherwise, be lent, resold, hired out, or otherwise circulated without the publisher's prior consent in any form of binding or cover other than that in which it is published and without a similar condition including this condition being imposed on the subsequent purchaser. Under no circumstances may any part of this book be photocopied for resale.

This is a work of fiction. Any similarity between the characters and situations within its pages and places or persons, living or dead, is unintentional and coincidental.

Published by Piper Lawson Books

Content editing by Becca Mysoor
Line and copy editing by Cassie Robertson
Proofreading by Devon Burke
Cover design by Emily Wittig

*For the girls
who were told to grow up
(and only smiled)*

1

NOVA

We all have dreams that light us up and turn us on.

Ones that make us tingle and come alive.

I didn't expect mine to become a reality.

And I never thought they'd look like *him*.

When I step onto the airplane, my heart pounding with anticipation, I expect to find business class bursting with glamorous people and enough legroom to lie down between rows.

There isn't room for a floor nap, but there are hand towels and bottled water.

I strap into 1B, then tuck my magazine and boarding pass into the pocket on the wall in front of me.

"Would you like a blanket?"

The flight attendant's perky voice has me straightening.

"I'm fine, thanks. Honestly, I could sweat in a snowstorm. I used to think it was a curse, but it's kind of a blessing."

She's staring at my pink flip-flops as if they might bite her.

"Please switch your phone to airplane mode for takeoff."

She continues down the rows.

My phone shows no new messages, so I send one.

Nova: Can't wait to see you! I can't believe this is really happening. Wish me luck :D

I switch the device off and twist the silver bangle on my wrist.

I'm on an adventure, I remind myself as I lean toward the window in time to see a plane lift off the tarmac.

My stomach flips.

This is why I got the aisle seat—so I'm as far as possible from watching *that*.

I open a note on my phone and reread what I've written.

Mari and I used to dress up as brides. We'd make dresses out of old tablecloths and toilet paper and race through the fields.

I'd run as fast as my legs would carry me, and she followed behind to make sure I didn't fall.

She'd roll her eyes and tell me I was being ridiculous, but I knew she loved me.

"How long until takeoff?" a woman across from me asks when the flight attendant passes the other direction.

"We're waiting on one more passenger."

I didn't realize planes waited on passengers.

Out the window, another plane races down the runway like a speeding bullet.

The shrill sound of a phone echoes in my mind, the only warning before darkness reaches for me, clawing up from deep in my stomach. Sweat beads at the back of my neck.

I've been talking myself into this for days.

But now...I'm not sure I can do it.

It's not too late to get off.

I'm halfway out of my seat when I collide with a man coming down the aisle.

He's huge, towering above me and easily engulfing the space around us with his broad shoulders and wall of a chest. His face is partially hidden by his hoodie while sweatpants cling to his lean hips and strong legs. A logo-print duffel is clutched firmly in his hand.

He glances into the overhead with a brief double-take at my pink luggage before dropping his bag at his feet and yanking off Beats headphones.

"You're in my seat."

His voice is more growl than words, and it rubs along my skin like sandpaper.

My fear is crowded out by disbelief at this man's audacity. "I don't think so. I'm 1B."

I checked my boarding pass a zillion times as I navigated the airport.

His eyes narrow. "I'm always 1B."

"Except today," I go on helpfully as I drop back into my aisle seat, which grew infinitely more appealing in the seconds since this stranger tried to take it from me.

I shift my knees to the side, the universal symbol for "go on through."

His stare is intense, and looking for a way out, I reach into the pocket for my boarding pass that's tucked in a magazine somewhere.

My bracelet slips halfway off, and I push it back on.

He doesn't move.

Finally, his impatience overwhelms me.

"Fine! If it matters so much to you, take it." I shift over to the window. Not my fault if I lose my breakfast on him. "We're waiting for a late arrival..."

I trail off as the flight attendant shuts the doors.

He's the late arrival.

He shoves his duffel into the overhead compartment and sinks into the seat, tugging his hood back from his head.

My breath catches.

His eyes are the color of chocolate, smoldering with little flecks of gold and fringed with thick lashes. A faded scar slices through one of his eyebrows. Almost-black hair decorates his square jaw, a five o' clock shadow though it's barely two. His nose has a slight dent, and his lips look as though they've been cut from marble.

Good God, he's beautiful.

Strikingly, imperfectly beautiful.

Picasso said the reason his portraits were skewed, why he painted every eye differently, is because every eye *is* different. It's not an issue of painting; it's an issue of *seeing*.

If uniqueness is beauty, this man is a work of art.

The pilot runs through the takeoff spiel, and the flight attendant demonstrates how to fasten a seatbelt. Her attention is fixed on the guy next to me, as if he's the one responsible for getting us to our destination in one piece.

"The flight over to Denver will be turbulent," the pilot says over the speaker.

I take a deep breath as I pull out my phone and switch on the signal.

Nothing from Mari.

I turn it off again and lean back against the headrest.

The engine starts, a rolling hum that vibrates through me.

"Do you take a lot of planes?" I ask.

My seatmate stares blankly.

"Is this one good? Safe?" I press.

He leans over me to look out the window. "Got two wings."

The plane starts its acceleration down the runway.

"I'm Nova," I manage as the plane lifts off.

Talking will keep my mind off our situation.

Hoodie Guy glances over but doesn't answer. He's a few years older than me, probably late twenties or early thirties.

No name. Got it.

"Are you from Denver?" I press.

"No."

"Me neither. I'm going for a wedding."

He exhales hard, as though resisting small talk is the noblest possible pastime and he considers himself a knight of the highest order.

"Work."

It's a grudging gift from lips so perfectly formed I'd trace them, if I didn't think he'd bite me first.

His knees nearly reach the opposite wall, even with the added legroom, while my feet barely touch the floor.

"Construction? Because you're huge," I go on at his expression. "Tall, I mean," I add as the woman across the aisle coughs. "Not huge other places."

His brows lift.

Now I'm looking at the hands folded across his

stomach. They're big, and tan, with long fingers and tidy nails.

Outside, the ground drops farther away. I force my attention away from the window.

"I've avoided flying for years now, but my sister is getting married and I won't let her down. In fact, I'm working on my speech right now. Do you want to hear—"

"I don't."

My mouth snaps shut.

If Mari was here, she'd tell me not to talk so much.

I flip my phone facedown in my lap and take a deep breath.

"I'm sorry. It's my nerves about flying. I'm trying not to have a panic attack. If I have to spend the entire flight curled in a ball on the floor, I will get there in one piece. I'd do anything for my sister. We'd do anything for each other," I finish in a single breath.

My seatmate frowns, studying me with a new intensity.

As if, for the first time, I'm something other than a nuisance.

He reaches across to lower the shade so I can't see the lack of ground firsthand.

The panic recedes a degree.

He's close, his faces inches from mine.

"Switch me seats," he says before I can thank him.

My heart beats faster as I reach for my seatbelt.

We switch spots, and his body brushes mine. I nearly trip. Sparks dance along my nerve endings.

He puts a steadying hand on my waist.

Only it's not steadying at all. It makes my stomach flutter in an entirely new way.

His hands are huge, and when I look down, tendrils of black ink like smudges of charcoal extend from under the cuffs of his sweatshirt.

What the...

They're mysterious and badass and more than a little hot.

My thighs press together.

I haven't thought about sex in weeks. Possibly months. Not since...

Well.

Let's just say what happens between the sheets has never blown my mind.

But between his massive build, the glittering dark eyes, and the intriguing secrets, this man is built for fantasies I never knew I had.

I don't normally go around thinking filthy thoughts about strangers, especially grouchy ones, but I sneak another look at those hands as he sits, adjusting his sweatpants over hard thighs and—

The flight attendant unclips from her seat and approaches. "Can I get you a drink, Mr.—"

"Tequila?" I ask hopefully.

It's fake courage, but I'll take whatever I can get.

My seatmate holds up two fingers.

The flight attendant nods so fast her neck cracks. Guess I'm not the only one noticing how attractive he is.

A few deep breaths later, she returns with the drinks.

"To new adventures." I lift my glass and then drink its contents back in a single shot, the heat burning down my throat.

He watches before drinking his in a long, slow gulp, his tanned throat bobbing.

I'm thirsty again.

The tequila's already working its magic, and the humming of the plane sounds farther away and less threatening. The alcohol has the not-unpleasant side effect of making my skin tingle.

"Do you like games?" I ask. "We could play one. Two Truths and a Lie. That's where I make three statements—"

"I know how to play."

My seatmate stacks our empty glasses and sets both on his tray.

I take that as assent and try to think up a good one. "I once stole a chocolate bar from a grocery store."

His beautiful mouth twists in dissatisfaction.

Lame.

"I once gave a man a tattoo."

Now there's a lift of one dark brow. He's

listening.

"And... I love my sister more than anyone in the world."

He makes a sound like a scoff as he takes me in, a long sweep from my toes upward that lingers on my faded jeans, the curve of my breasts under my off-the-shoulder T-shirt, and my candy-pink hair before landing on the lip gloss I swear the tequila washed away.

I'm not a total stranger to male attention. But I've never been the subject of a look like that, and certainly not from a man like him.

"The last one."

My mouth falls open in protest. "What? Why would I lie about that?"

"You're not lying to me. You're lying to yourself."

What the...? Did this guy I've known for fifteen minutes seriously question my relationship with my sister?

The flight attendant returns, like a magnet who's found her true north, and my hoodie hottie orders us two more tequilas.

The first is going to my head, like helium lifting me up.

The drinks are set in front of us moments later with another longing look at Mr. Grumpy, plus a suspicious one at me. She's perturbed I'm building rapport with her dream guy.

Funny how being in a confined space with

another person, in the presence of alcohol, breaks down boundaries.

I take a sip, trying his method of pacing consumption, and make a face.

It tastes terrible.

I toss the rest back in a single swig and set the cup on my tray with a flourish.

"Your turn to say three things," I inform him.

"No."

"That's how games work."

"'How games work' is you should know the rules before you start."

He reaches for his phone and starts reading.

Well then.

I fish in the seat pocket and take out my magazine. *Sports Illustrated.*

My companion glances over. His eyes stick to the magazine.

"My new brother-in-law, he's—" I catch myself, remembering my sister's request to be discrete. According to Mari, Harlan's some hotshot basketball GM, and I shouldn't announce that to everyone. "He's really into sports."

He looks over my shoulder, then rips the open page out of the magazine.

He crumples it in his fist and shoves it in his seat pocket.

My jaw hits the floor.

"Just because you're not into sports doesn't mean it's not a viable interest for others."

Apparently, tequila has the side effect of giving me a soapbox and whispering that I should use it.

"That so."

I survey his tall physique, admittedly a bit too happy to have an excuse to stare at his long, hard legs, his impossibly broad shoulders, his huge hands.

"You ever play basketball? I bet you'd be good."

His mouth twitches. A sign of life. "I'll keep that in mind."

He reaches for his headphones and tugs his hoodie back up over his head.

Guess we're done talking.

For the next hour, I read my magazine and sneak looks at him while he plays around on his phone.

I wish I had a sketchpad.

I don't typically draw people, but I'm itching to draw him.

It's not only the beautiful lines of his face and body, larger than anyone I've ever seen in person. It's his magnetic charisma, which is twisted because he couldn't give more standoffish vibes if his sweatshirt had "STAY AWAY" printed from cuff to collar.

A few times, I catch him looking at me.

It's like being scorched by the sun. Not sunbathing-on-a-beach sun, but ant-under-a-microscope sun. I'm not used to his intensity, but I don't hate having his eyes on me.

I remind myself of the purpose of this trip.

My sister and I were close growing up. Even when she moved to Denver, we talked every few days and spent holidays together.

I didn't realize how much distance was between us until I got the invitation saying she was getting married to a man I'd never met.

The second I got the invitation, I called and told her I was coming to help.

For the next month, I'm in Denver for her wedding. We haven't talked about exactly what I'll be doing, but I've already had visions of us hugging, our flower bouquets wrapped around one another's shoulders, and the happy tears in her eyes when I give the world's best MOH speech.

It's not like Mari's all I have in the world, but... well, she sort of is.

An announcement comes over the intercom to say we'll be landing in Denver in an hour.

Not soon enough.

The plane bounces, and my stomach lurches. I unclick my seatbelt and stumble out of my seat toward the bathroom.

I was hoping to avoid the "rocking in a corner" scenario, but it seems more likely with every bump.

"I'm sorry, Mar," I whisper.

I brace a hand on the counter and think of my childhood hero. My partner in crime.

Every time my life has gone to shit, she's been the

one who got me through. I want to return the favor. To be there when she needs me instead of the other way around.

A knock comes on the door, making it clank against the frame. Apparently, I forgot to lock it.

The door opens, and my seatmate is there, staring down at me with his trademark irritated expression. "What's wrong?"

"I can't do this," I whisper as I squeeze my eyes shut. "I can't..."

I expect him to signal for the flight attendant to come get the crazy woman rocking in the bathroom.

Instead, he wedges inside along with me.

It's barely big enough for both of us. His legs brush mine, his knees resting against my thighs as the plane bumps and jolts.

"Oh God," I whisper, squeezing my eyes shut.

"My friends call me Clay, but I'll take it."

I force my eyes open to find him looming over me. His expression is composed, except for the flecks of gold dancing in those moody eyes.

He shoves up his sleeves, revealing muscled arms covered in tattoos. The stunning patterns of black inked across smooth, tanned skin make me gasp.

"These are amazing." I whisper like I'm in a church.

The panic recedes enough for me to take his wrist, trace the parallel lines that begin to twist and intersect midway up his forearm.

He tenses at first, but doesn't pull away.

"How many do you have?" I ask.

"Twenty-nine." His voice is softer than it was before. "One for every year I've been alive."

On his other arm, there's a pine tree, tall and strong with thinning branches near the top.

"You got your first tattoo when you were a baby?"

I only realize how dumb that sounds once it's out.

But instead of calling me out, his eyes crease at the corners. "I doubled up a few years."

He looks different when he's half-smiling. I wonder what it would take to make him smile for real.

"I always wanted one, but it was never the right time," I say as I refocus on the tattoos. It feels safer than staring into his eyes.

The plane hits a bump, and my stomach lurches.

Clay tenses. He's going to bail on me before I embarrass myself more by puking on him.

Instead, he reaches back and yanks the hoodie off over his head.

My heart stops.

He's a canvas, a work of art. Like one of those *I Spy* books I had as a kid, except every tattoo is a masterpiece.

The body revealed by his white tank is as impressive as his tattoos. Beneath the ink, he's another kind of art. Every inch of shredded muscle and smooth skin makes me wonder what he does, what he's capable of doing.

I take a breath and focus on the lines and not the fact that we're millimeters apart.

He shows me a tattoo riding the crest of his shoulder, a hawk. I've barely absorbed that when I notice the black snake disappearing under his tank.

The hammering in my ears is still there, but it feels like I'm creating it instead of being its victim.

It's as if, in this tiny excuse for a room on a bouncing metal tube, I'm safe with him so long as we're breathing together.

"This one's the newest." He points to the rabbit on his wrist. "It's for my sister. She can be a pain in the ass, but I like knowing she's with me."

It's a gruff admission, but suddenly, emotions rise up that I can't contain. Ones that have nothing to do with planes and bumps.

"You were right." I swallow hard. "Things have been strained between us. I was dating this guy, and we moved in together, and he dumped me and I got fired the same day, and I haven't told my sister any of it because she lives this perfect life. Now she's marrying some guy I've never met, and I need the month leading up to this wedding to show her I can be a good sister."

Overhead, the yellow-orange lights make a halo around him.

He grabs my chin and swipes at the tears I didn't feel drying on my cheeks.

"You're doing something you hate for someone you love. You're already a good sister."

This room is too small, and he's too big, and I feel the distance between us as much as the places we're touching. He smells like soap and forest, like the pine tree on his arm.

My stomach is forgotten as the vibe shifts between us. The negative space is humming, throbbing. It's not fear or panic anymore, the fundamental need to be apart from this plane.

It's a pull toward him.

And I'm not the only one feeling it. I see it on his face, in the flaring of his nostrils, the tic of his jaw.

"Tell you what, Pink." His voice is a gravely rasp that ends between my thighs, even before I can process the nickname. "We make it out of here, I owe you a tattoo."

I'm suddenly aware of how close we are. How alone, despite the hundreds of people on the other side of the flimsy door.

He feels a little dangerous, but a good kind of danger.

My breath catches. "For real?"

He bends to my ear, his lips brushing my skin. "I promise."

My entire body is humming with arousal and possibility.

Once, as a kid, I accidentally scraped my knee until it was bloody. Seeing the skin grow back was fascinating. That's what this feels like—like he's touching me but a new part of me. A part I'm not sure is ready to be touched.

I fist the front of his tank, my hand disappearing in soft cotton. The little sound I make is part moan, part sigh.

Everything goes black.

When I blink my eyes open, I'm back in my seat and have no idea how I got there.

I must have fallen asleep for landing because the plane is pulled up to the gate and passengers are dragging suitcases up the aisle.

The seat next to me is empty, the duffel and its owner long gone.

"Excuse me," I ask the flight attendant as I wipe at the corner of my mouth. "What happened to the man who was sitting here?"

She looks at me as if I'm nuts.

2

NOVA

"There you are. They didn't say you'd be delayed. Did you lose weight?" Mari demands.

I throw my arms around her. "I missed you, too."

After landing, I rushed through the terminal, my pink bag in tow, eager to reunite with my sister.

Now, she pulls back to study me and touches my faded pink strands, a contrast to her bright platinum ones. "Harlan had some business at the airport, but he'll find us at the car."

"You've still never told me how you met," I say as we walk.

"At a work party six months ago. We were doing PR for a charity, and he was there on behalf of the Kodiaks, his new team."

"And now you're getting married." I shake my head.

"Don't sound so shocked. He's insanely accomplished. He loves me. And he cries at sad movies." She waves as she spots the tall man hanging up his phone and striding across the arrivals lounge. "I thought we were meeting at the car."

"Two beautiful ladies. I couldn't wait."

"Nova, this is Harlan."

His grin is quick and welcoming. Every part of him, from the tailored button-down to the firm handshake, says he's comfortable with himself and good at making other people feel comfortable, too.

"Nova. I've heard lots about you."

"I've heard almost nothing about you," I admit.

Mari gasps, but he only laughs.

The way he rests his hand on her back is familiar and sweet, and there's a pang in my gut.

They look fantastic together. He's handsome and polished in gray dress pants a soft mauve shirt that looks beautiful against his golden skin. She's tall and curvy, wearing dark trousers and a soft sweater in the same shade that seems somehow cooler than black. The freckles that used to come out in the summer are gone, or covered by foundation.

Any reservation I feel is protectiveness over my sister. I never thought she'd fall this hard this fast.

We head toward the arrivals area, where a sleek Mercedes waits.

"The issues resolved for tomorrow's practice?" Mari asks.

"Not quite." Harlan puts my bag in the back before rounding to the driver's door.

Mari sighs. "Can't you cut him loose?"

"He's an all-star, Mar."

"He's going to ruin your life."

Harlan clears his throat as they shift into the front seats and I take the back.

"Enough shop talk. We'll bore Nova," he says as we pull away, reminding Mari I'm here.

"That's true. The closest she got to sports as a kid was hopscotch. She was always doodling and daydreaming."

"Hey!" I protest.

"One time in school, they asked what she was going to be when she grew up, and she said a unicorn."

"It was cute," I weigh in.

"You were twelve."

We make conversation, Harlan asking enough questions that I barely get in any of my own.

I tell him how long I've been living in Boston, that the only pet I have is a goldfish named Samson whom a friend is watching for the month I'm here, and that I've worked the past year since graduating college as an administrative assistant at an interior design firm.

"Here we are," Mari says as we turn into a neighborhood full of grand houses and rolling hills. The lush landscape is bedecked with manicured lawns and perfectly kept gardens.

"Cherry Hills Village," I read off the sign, taking it all in with wide eyes.

We pull up in front of a house perched on a hill with a killer view, and we get out of the car.

The grounds are a paradise, green and full of life, stylishly landscaped to perfection, with a pond in the back nestled amongst blue spruces and bur oak trees.

"We're still getting used to living together," Harlan says. "Fortunately, when we fight, we have five acres to get away from each other."

I smile. It's impossible not to like this man. He's warm and self-deprecating.

"We really appreciate you dropping everything to come for a month," he goes on.

"It wasn't a problem with work?" Mari asks.

"Not at all."

They told me to stay away.

"Then this will be a break before you head back in the fall." Harlan nods without waiting for me to contradict him.

Mari frowns as if the idea of a break is worrisome, but her fiancé continues.

"We're so pleased you can stay with us. But as we're out of the city, you'll be needing a way to get around. I'll lend you a car." He points toward the garage, and I count five doors.

"There's no way that's full," I gasp.

He rubs a hand over his head, sheepish, and excitement has my heart pounding.

I haven't had my own car in... ever.

We head toward the front of the stunning house.

I notice again how tall Harlan is as he pushes open the front door and waits for Mari and me to go first.

Suddenly, Clay is back in my mind. The dark eyes, the huge hands, the tattoos.

Mari leans in. "I'm surprised Brad let you come this early. How is he?"

Her words slice through my daydream. "I'm not sure. It feels like I never see him."

"He must be busy being a principle at the firm. It'll be good to catch up with him at the wedding."

A ribbon of guilt wraps around my stomach. I ignore it and flash a smile. "Are you going to give me a tour or what?"

"And this is your room."

Mari finishes our walk of the palatial house at a doorway on the second floor.

It's big and bright with an en-suite bathroom that makes my jaw drop. "There are two shower heads."

"Go nuts."

I throw my arms around her shoulders. "I'm really glad I'm here."

She inhales. "Me, too. Though I didn't expect you to come for an entire month. I can't take a month off work, and I'm the one getting married."

"Guess I'm just lucky."

I reach for the bracelet on my wrist before realizing it's not there.

Dammit.

"What's wrong?" she asks.

"I... Nothing."

It must be on the plane somewhere. In the bathroom or wedged in between the seats.

No.

Mari's phone buzzes. "I need to get some work done tonight to prove I'm relevant before I disappear for two weeks."

After Mari leaves, I lift my pink suitcase onto the bed.

I dig out my jewelry box and set it on the wardrobe, lifting the lid.

Inside are necklaces, earrings, fun things from thrift stores.

No bracelet.

It wasn't fancy, just a simple bangle, but it was my mom's.

I can't believe I was distracted enough that I lost it.

My chest tightens as my gaze lands on another piece of jewelry.

I shut the box lid quickly and turn back to my bags.

Maybe I didn't put the bracelet on today.

It's possible I was drunk on the flight. My memories are blurry.

Blurry enough to forget what I was wearing?

Blurry enough to hallucinate a seat mate and our entire conversation?

I unpack my carry-on, putting folded clothes in the empty dresser, then reach for the front zipper.

Feeling in the front pocket for anything I missed, I hit glossy paper, tightly bound. I pull out the *Sports Illustrated*. When I open it, it falls open to the ripped-out page.

I trace the jagged edge and think of his warm eyes.

His strong hands.

His tattoos.

I bite my lip.

He's real.

It felt so good. His touch, his attention. The way he looked at me as if he saw me.

But I'll never see him again.

Which is good because I'm here for my sister, and a fresh start. The last thing I need is to be distracted by some gorgeous guy from a different world.

I drop the magazine on the wardrobe next to the jewelry box and resolve to forget him.

3

CLAY

"This is going to be embarrassing for you," I growl.

"Try it." Jay's down in a defensive stance, eyes tracking my every move as though he's a snake charmer and I'm a cobra.

"You're not ready."

"I was ready yesterday." He reaches to try to snatch the ball midair from between my knees, and I pull my dribble tighter and grin.

"You waiting for retirement?" He demands, shaking his head and making his braids sway. "Come on."

It's a game within a game. The one-on-one battle of strategy, agility, and strength between offense and defence.

Jay might be one of the top guards in the world, but I'm one of the top scorers.

And I hate to lose.

He's half a second late, and I weave past him, driving to the basket.

Atlas comes off his man to cover me, his icy eyes intent.

Miles waves. "I'm open!"

The basket looms just past Atlas's fingertips.

I take the step back.

Swish.

The other guys on the court all groan, and I shake my head at Jay. "You can't guard me."

My friend and teammate rolls his eyes. "Missed you this summer, too, man. Now, let's see you do it again."

We run another play that ends with the ball in the basket off my fingertips.

Swish.

There's nothing like the feeling of the perfect shot. From the second the ball leaves your fingers, you know.

It's physics.

Music.

Poetry.

Every subject I didn't give a shit about in school.

Swish.

Not a lot you can count on in this world, but the perfect arc of that ball from your fingertips when you've done it a million times before...

That's the real deal.

Jay tries to wrench the ball from my hands.

"Foul!" Miles shouts.

"Like hell," Jay bites out.

I dribble around Jay to find Atlas, our center and the biggest guy on our roster, on the other side.

"You wanna take me?" I ask.

His half-hearted defense makes me smirk as I dodge around him, hitting a point-blank layup before the whistle sounds.

"Wade!" Coach barks. "We got a week until preseason. How many men you see on this court?"

"Coach, you know Clay dropped math in college." Miles laughs, fist-bumping me.

"The game isn't one-on-one. I know you've been injured half a season, but now that you're back, they'll be sending bodies at you. Get Rookie involved."

We set up to run it again.

Seeing the guys again after a couple months feels good. The advantage of being a senior member of the team is skipping training camp. They trust you to prep your game and be ready to work when you land.

Literally.

I got off the plane and just had time to drop my bags at my place before driving to practice.

An interesting flight it was, too—

"Clay!" Miles shouts as he passes to me, nearly taking off my head.

I react in time and catch the ball, lob it across to

Rookie, then cut behind the guy covering him. Rookie sends it back to me for a dunk.

Hollers go up from around the court.

But this time, when I land, my knee twinges.

I grit my teeth to hide my response to the pain.

Coach blows his whistle before anyone notices.

At first, I think he's going to let us go, but then I spot the figure approaching from the bleachers.

I straighten, palming the ball as I take in the familiar form.

"Gather 'round," Harlan calls.

I shake my head before turning to our new GM.

"There's no mincing words. It's my first full season here, and I want to win a championship," Harlan says.

"You've got a ring already," Jayden jokes.

The guys laugh.

"There's a reason we're having the wedding before opening day. This team is my priority for this year. Basketball is a family. It's easy to put your own wants ahead of others, but at the end of the day, we need other people in order to succeed."

Bullshit.

I turn and grab the black bag with my phone and personal shit on my way toward the tunnel.

"Clay!" Jay calls.

I pretend not to hear him.

It's fake. Every word from Harlan's mouth.

"You're making this harder than it needs to be.

On you and everyone else," Harlan calls, catching up to me.

I drop my half-open bag between my feet. Sweat drips off my face and lands between my Kobes on the polished floor. "You think I don't care about basketball?"

"You care more than anyone I've ever met. It's why this team went to the effort to trade for you despite your baggage."

I snort. "If you were part of this team when the trade came up, I would've passed."

I keep my game dialed so the rest doesn't bleed in. Except...

A flash of neon pink catches my eye.

It's only a staffer wheeling a cart of colored basketballs for some charity thing at the other end of the hall.

Still, the sight drags me back to the plane, and the girl whose hair was the same color.

Nova.

The pixie sitting in my seat who said more in an hour than I say all day. Cute and bright, the kind of cheerful that tries to rub off on you when you're not looking. Even when I tried to shut her down, she persisted.

She didn't know who I was. Can't recall the last time I felt so invisible.

At first, it was entertaining, but after a while, it was liberating.

I could be anyone, do anything I wanted.

A hollowness has lingered in my chest ever since I arrived here in Denver last year. An emptiness or a dissatisfaction or both that I can't talk about, let alone square with, because I'm living a life most people only dream of.

But when she looked up at me with those indigo eyes, trusting and vulnerable and talking about how she was gonna go to the wall for her sister, I felt something tugging on my heartstrings for the first time in years.

Harlan's voice brings me back. "You're one of the best players I've ever seen, Wade. You can make this team win. But your stock isn't as high as it was. You're coming off an injury, and even if you weren't, you can't do this alone."

I grab a sweat towel out of my bag, wiping my neck.

"Save your breath. Don't pretend to be my friend or whatever the new management technique is—we're not friends. You made sure of that years ago."

I ball up the fabric and shoot it into the used towel bin half a dozen feet away before continuing down the hall toward the locker room.

4

NOVA

"Oh God, yes."

My praise echoes off the walls of the bathroom.

The shower is every bit as decadent as it looked. The water pressure is like a massage, and the heat is amazing.

I bounded out of bed at six thanks to the time difference. The flight is behind me, and so is everything from my past life.

Back home, I might have a complicated work and relationship status, but in Denver, I'm about to help my sister have the most incredible wedding and maybe create a new version of myself at the same time.

When I stepped into the shower, I let the warm water cascade over my body, washing away the grime of a long day of travel.

Now my fingertips graze my skin, following my curves.

Without permission, my growly plane hottie appears in front of me.

His dark eyes and messy hair. The way he looked at me made my skin tingle. The way he spoke to me made me feel…

Real.

Alive.

Seen.

I haven't had an orgasm in weeks, but something about yesterday has me on edge, and it wasn't only the flight.

Suddenly, Clay looms over me, huge and hard and deliberate. His gaze lingers on me with a heat that burns through my skin.

He lifts me in his arms, pressing my back against the shower tile while he slides his massive length between my thighs.

He whispers how I'm a good sister, a good person, and when I tell him I'm actually bad, he says he likes me both ways.

I trail my fingertips over my slick skin until my body tightens and quivers.

Waves of pleasure radiate through me and leave me gasping in the aftershocks.

"It will be nice to see Brad at the wedding."

Mari's voice slices into my thoughts.

I stick my head under the spray and let it wash

away the reminder of the secret filling the space between us.

After showering and drying my hair, I tug on jean shorts and a fresh white T-shirt that skims my body before heading downstairs.

I find Mari in the kitchen making coffee.

It's barely six thirty, and she's already polished in a pant suit and heels. My sister is five years older, but sometimes it feels like a lifetime.

"You ever think you'd have this after the trailer?" I tease, coming up behind her.

She turns and does a once-over of my outfit. "That's why I busted my ass to get through school and work my way up at the agency. I wanted a place to call home. Somewhere with flowers planted in the ground that you could see year after year."

"But we saw new flowers every year," I point out.

She rolls her eyes. "It wasn't only the flowers, Nova."

We've seen a lot of the country thanks to our parents raising us on the road and homeschooling us. They said there was no point staying in one place, preferring to drift from one community to another. After they died, I always ran to Mari for help. She had her shit together from the time we were kids. No weaknesses or cracks.

"I can't believe there's still so much to do in less than a month," she frets.

"Put me to work. That's why I came early. I want to be useful. I can run errands."

Yesterday, Harlan showed me the cavernous garage, complete with five shiny luxury vehicles. He offered me my choice of two, and I picked a sleek silver Volvo.

"That would be great. But it might be smart for you to check in with your office, too, while you're here," she says pointedly.

"Not necessary. I mean," I go on at her expression, "I'll give it a few days first. So they have time to miss me."

I mostly want to forget about it and focus on my sister.

"Oh! You haven't shown me your dress," I say to distract her from serious things.

Mari pulls out her phone and shows me the photos of herself at the designer's boutique. "It's getting taken in as we speak. Now I just have to put nothing in my mouth for the next thirty days."

The dress is sleek and sexy, chic lines and clinging lace. "I thought you were getting an A-line with a huge train."

"Mermaid style is more sophisticated."

"But you wanted a princess gown."

"When I was ten, Nova." She laughs.

We used to dress up as brides as little girls. We'd pull wildflowers from near the camper we lived in to make bouquets and use mosquito netting for veils.

Being on the road, we didn't have a lot of possessions, but it never bothered me. We made our own joy from the things around us.

I shake it off.

"So, I can't wait to get started. Tell me what you need."

"The guests are confirmed, obviously. The venue is secured, and we're doing the reception here at the house. Flowers are ordered, and there's a cake testing scheduled in a couple of days, but..."

My heart leaps at the prospect of helping in some important way.

"We need to approve the linens for dinner, which means getting fabric swatches over to Chloe."

"Who's Chloe?"

"Chloe Kim is Harlan's head of PR. And my maid of honor."

The twisting in my gut is sharp as my vision of standing at my sister's side comes crashing down.

I think of the MOH speech I've been working on. The imagined pictures of us together with matching bouquets.

Sure, my sister didn't officially ask me to be her MOH, or hint that she would, but I figured everything was last minute.

"Oh." I force a smile and pretend I'm not dying inside. "I can't wait to meet her."

"You'll love her. You'll get a chance to talk to her at the dress fitting in a few days."

And agonize over what Chloe has that I don't until then?

Hard pass.

"Hey, what if I run those samples over to Chloe now? Save you the stress."

Mari's brows lift. "Great. Let me text her."

∼

Don't spill on this car.

I carefully navigate the Starbucks drive-through.

This is what they created ventis for: facing the woman who's replaced you at your sister's side.

Once it's tucked into the cupholder, I follow my phone's navigation to the Denver Kodiaks' stadium in the heart of town.

Security helps me find parking when I flash my ID.

No matter who Chloe is, I'm going to make this wedding the best it can be. Nothing will get in the way.

I take a sip of Starbucks to ease the knot in my chest.

Inside, the stadium is next level.

My feet seem to echo in the vast hallways, empty except for security at their posts. One of the guards points the way to a black-and-purple reception desk. On the wall is a huge logo of a growling bear with a basketball, and two women are behind the desk, conferring.

"Hi! I'm Lena, Chloe's assistant." One of the women springs forward, beaming when she spots me. "You must be Nova. Have you seen the court? We can stop by on the way to Chloe's office."

She leads me through the halls, including a detour down a dark hallway that opens into the vast arena.

I love learning new things and going new places, and this feels like a different world. I've been to one pro hockey game, plus lots of concerts, mostly with cheap tickets, except the time I won lower bowl in a contest.

It's fascinating to see the stadium from down here.

The rows of seats seem to go for miles. There's a faint smell of cleaning supplies and rubber.

On the court, players are working out.

The team is running drills, half the guys in purple and the others in gold.

"The bench and rookies have extra practice once this wraps up," Lena explains. "The starters will go lift. Their focus is on getting stronger and tougher."

My attention is drawn to one player in particular. In the sea of jerseys, his is purple, and he looks stronger, bigger, faster than the others. His arms are covered in tattoos. There's something about the way he moves…

"Who's your favorite?" she asks, motioning me to follow.

I snap out of it and comply.

"I don't really follow basketball." My host's eyes widen. "How about you?"

Lena smiles dreamily as we pass a wall of jerseys.

Wade.

Issa.

Griffin.

Brooks.

Lopez.

"Wade, all the way. Me and every other girl in Denver, right?"

"Why him?" I ask to make conversation as we wind through more hallways with glass walls. The conference rooms and offices have names etched into them.

"He's gorgeous and broody and talented. I met him once in the hall, and I couldn't even speak. I think I got pregnant from the eye contact though."

She winks and I laugh.

Eventually, we stop in front of an office, and a woman who's probably late twenties like Mari waves from inside. She's wearing a moss-green skirt suit, a nod to corporate and the scenery, her dark hair sleek over her shoulders. Her assistant gestures me inside the office and leaves.

"No. Tell him we're doing this my way, or I'll shred his press badge." She stabs a button on her phone and shakes her head. Her eyes land on me and brighten. "You must be Nova."

I shake her hand. "Because you're expecting me or because I look like Mari?"

"The former. You look nothing like your sister." Chloe's laugh is warmer than I expect. I hand her the samples, and she thanks me, setting them on her desk. "How's your coffee?"

"Half full."

"We'll go grab another. I need to stretch my legs."

"You're the head of PR for the team," I say as we start down the hall in the other direction. "You look so young."

Chloe winks. "Tell my parents that. I didn't become a doctor, so they were bummed. We're working it out slowly and over many dinners."

Dammit. She's not only smart and pretty—she's nice.

We weave past rooms and corridors, her heels clicking the entire way. She waves to people as we pass.

"I bet you were the perfect child," I say.

"I was a tomboy. Grew up playing basketball. My older brothers played, too. Eventually, we stopped playing together though."

"They were too good?"

"I was too rough. One nasty elbow to the groin and my brother called it quits."

When she smiles, I do, too. It's like we have a secret together.

"Listen, I know you're Mari's MOH, and I respect that, but it's obvious you're busy. I want to help any way I can," I offer.

Chloe's face splits into an appreciative smile.

"That would be great, thank you. Most of the big pieces are done, but there is the bachelorette. I was thinking of having it at a spa, about a week out so it's not a stressful rush right before."

"I love that! Maybe we can bring treats and our own decorations," I go on.

We keep chatting until we get to the kitchen, and Chloe makes me a cappuccino. "It's not Miles's, but it's something."

"Who's Miles?"

She cocks her head. "You a basketball fan?"

"Not really."

"Perfect. This place can get pretty incestuous. Not to objectify the guys, but they're larger than life. Literally. It's easy to get seduced, whether they're trying to draw you into their orbit or not."

I blink. "You have nothing to worry about."

I'm coming off a breakup, and the only guy who made my vagina flutter was a stranger on a plane I'll never see again.

We head back toward her office but go a different way. At a bank of windows, I pull up. On the other side of the glass is a gym with sleek machines and free weights. Half a dozen guys are in there. They're tall and muscled, intent on their work.

"Enjoy from a distance," Chloe says. "They lift after practice. Preseason they're here for three or four hours a day, ramping up for all of the madness of the regular season. Then the other things start up—forty-plus games on the road, media availabilities. I give them a hard time, but these guys work their asses off."

Chloe's phone buzzes. "One second, Nova. Someone skipped a photoshoot." Her shiny hair slips over her shoulders as she shakes her head.

She turns away and speaks into her phone.

I go back to watching the guys work out. One in particular catches my eye. He's shirtless and lying on a bench, holding a barbell with impossibly huge plates on either end that he presses with the regularity of a drumbeat.

My throat dries at the physicality of it, the sheer strength and will required.

It's raw, beautiful, forceful.

But I'm not watching his shoulders or straining pecs.

I'm watching the tattoos. There must be a dozen or more. Black and covering swaths of his arms, his chest, his sides.

They're not only beautiful—they're familiar.

My heart stops.

It's him.

Clay.

The man I swore I'd never see again is working out in my BIL's building with the Kodiaks.

Scratch that, I realize as he sits up and wipes himself off with a jersey.

He's one of them.

5

CLAY

"There's no way you'll break the points record," Jay says.

"The only stat line you'll be breaking is the minutes record because you won't let Coach drag your ass off the court," Miles retorts.

"You assholes spotting me?" I grit out at the top of a rep. Sweat rolls off my forehead.

They glance down. "We are," they chorus in unison.

Three.

Every part of my chest contracts.

Two.

My arms shake.

One.

I exhale hard as the barbell clanks back into its cups. As the sweat rolls down my neck, it doesn't escape me that we're the only ones left in the gym.

"Where's Rookie? And the rest of the team?"

"Cleared out a few minutes ago," Jay answers. "They put in a solid practice today."

"Rookie's better than solid. The one thing you getting hurt last year did was get us a prime pick in the draft." Miles slaps my chest, grinning.

My lip curls.

Wasn't my plan to get hurt, for the team to tank. Before that, I thought we'd have a shot here.

It's a good group of guys. Jay likes to run his mouth, but he's talented and reliable. We played against each other in the same division in college. He's had my back through tough spots.

Miles is from Iowa and a couple years younger. We only crossed paths once in the Final Four of March Madness, but he's solid and loyal to a fault.

"You catch Harlan's media this morning?" Miles asks.

I sit up and shake my head, and Jay nods.

"He's playing it close to the vest about his plans for the team," Jay says.

"Seems pretty obvious to me," Miles weighs in. "He wants to build around you and Rookie."

I cut a look at my friend. "He talk to you?"

Jay lifts a shoulder. "Not really."

Harlan being brought in by ownership to manage the team at the end of last season wasn't part of the deal.

If I'd known sooner, I would've been gone before training camp.

On the surface, like any GM with something to prove, he wants to win.

But there's something underneath.

I wipe the sweat off before I reach for a new towel. The hairs lift on my neck, and I look through the glass.

There's Chloe on the phone, plus a girl.

One with pink hair and a curvy figure and...

Everything slows down.

Fuck me.

It's *her*.

The girl from the plane.

I've only been thinking about her for the past twenty-four hours, and here she is.

Before I can take a breath, she topples to the floor in a mass of limbs.

"Whoa, is she okay?" Miles asks.

I reach the door in three strides.

Outside, she's picking herself up. Her denim shorts show off long, curvy legs. Her white T-shirt is soaking up dark roast as she grabs for a fallen mug.

When she straightens, shoving a hand through her messy hair, her bright blue eyes lock on mine.

Her face fills with a thousand emotions. Shock. Awareness. Something I can't read but want to.

"Hi," she murmurs.

"Hi," I say.

She looks even younger than she did on the plane. A college student, or a recent graduate.

"Can you hold?" Chloe says into her phone before punching a button and turning to us. "You okay?"

Nova clutches the cup as if holding it will save it from falling the first time. "Great."

"Nova, this is Clay. Our star player. Clay, this is Nova, Harlan's future sister-in-law."

Cue record scratch.

No fucking way.

Did she know who I was when we met? I've seen people do some wild things to get my attention.

Except she's as stunned as me.

Chloe turns to Nova. "I have to finish this call. If you give me one second, I'll take you back to the kitchen to clean up."

"I'll take her."

I start down the hall without waiting for Nova or Chloe to agree.

The kitchen is mercifully quiet, holding just a couple of back-office staff who nod as we enter.

There are a million things I could say to her. Ask what she's doing here. If she's thought about me since the plane. Whether I'm imprinted on her brain like she's pressed her way into mine.

I settle on, "So, your sister's marrying Harlan."

She huffs out a little breath. "And you work for him."

"Wouldn't put it like that."

I wet a paper towel, intending to use it on the coffee stain on her shirt until my attention lands on her breasts.

"How would you put it?"

My gaze snaps back up, and I hand her the towel instead.

"Stars make the team," I say as she goes to work on it with vigor. "Harlan gets the brightest he can afford."

"Meaning you."

I cock my head. "I'm the brightest in the league."

Her groan is surprisingly guttural for such a small person. "And I said you should try basketball."

Oh, yeah, this day is taking a turn for the better.

"You were right."

"Ugh." She tugs on her hair, agonized. It's strangely endearing.

Before I can decide whether to laugh or just watch her some more, she looks straight at me with those bright blue eyes.

"Don't say anything," she pleads, cutting a look at the door. "About the stuff I said about my sister or about us meeting."

I'm still trying to understand what's going on in her head when something furry brushes my legs.

"There you are." Miles calls from the doorway, not waiting for an invitation. His gaze lands on Nova.

"Hey there. I'm Miles, and this is Waffles." He gestures to the French bulldog sniffing my shoe.

"Nova." She shakes his hand.

"What were you drinking?"

"Cappuccino," she says.

"Leave it to me."

Nova smiles for the first time.

Except she's smiling at him, not me.

"Clay thinks he's smooth with that 'I do my talking on the court' bullshit, but he's only an all-star troublemaker," Miles says as he turns to the espresso machine.

This time, she laughs.

It's musical, and my chest tightens.

When she bends down to pet the dog, I swallow the groan.

Jesus, I just got jock-blocked by a Frenchie.

I'm not standing around playing reserve to my shooting guard and his pint-sized dog.

I turn on my heel and head down the hall, willing the sound to stop echoing in my ears.

"Who's the girl?" Jay asks when I get to the changeroom.

"GM's sister-in-law." I burrow in my locker for a change of clothes.

He whistles. "You chase that, I don't care how many points you score—you'll get sent to detention."

"As much as I'd like to see Harlan try, I'm not planning on it."

"I figured," he says.

"Why's that?"

My friend shrugs.

"You don't do complications."

"You're right. I don't."

I grab a new shirt off a shelf and stalk down the hall to the kitchen.

They're standing close. Miles is tugging a jersey over her head.

"Screw paper towel. That'll cover a venti's worth of stains," he jokes.

"There's smoke coming from the coffee machine," I say coolly.

"Shit!" Miles spins like I told him his dog was on fire instead of circling the kitchen happily, chasing its stuffed frog toy.

Chloe paces in the doorway, still on the phone but eyeing the three of us with suspicion.

"He's serious about his coffee," Nova murmurs.

"Barista is his fallback career. His shooting doesn't improve soon, he's gonna need it," I say.

Her lips twitch, her eyes dancing.

My teammates and I regularly joke around and throw one another under the bus, but even if we didn't, I'd roast every damn one of them to make her smile.

"Here you go, Nova!" Miles is back, stretching a hand between us to hold out a coffee cup with frothed milk on top. He proudly displays his craftsmanship.

"Is that a basketball?" Nova asks, delighted.

Guy thinks he's Michel-fucking-angelo.

On the court, I pull rank every day of the week.

It's not like I'm trying to get with her.

But I saw her first.

I *met* her first.

I held her in an airplane bathroom while she hyperventilated.

She takes a sip and coos her approval.

"Stop sniffing around Nova. She's family," Chloe calls.

"Yeah, Waffles, stop sniffing around Nova." Miles winks before returning to the espresso machine to make another concoction.

I want to hit him.

Jay's right. I don't date. I'm basketball first, second, always.

The occasional hookup to blow off steam is one thing, but love fucks with your head. I couldn't afford it when I was healthy, not to mention now that I'm staging a comeback.

But I can't stop looking at her like she's a rainbow in the middle of a storm.

Chloe leans into the kitchen.

"Sorry, Nova. Let's go."

"Nice to meet you, Nova," Miles calls. "You need a tour guide, you know where to find me."

"Thanks." Nova looks back at me for a moment. "Nice to meet you, Clay."

"Wait." I grab Nova's hand and a marker off the counter and open her palm.

"What are you doing?" she murmurs.

Her skin is soft, and I try not to think too hard about the way her fingers curl around mine.

"I promised you a tattoo," I mutter under my breath, reminding her of my vow on the plane.

Her mouth falls open as I write across her hand. "That's my tattoo?"

"No. It's how you redeem it."

She bites her lip and closes her hand.

I don't have to watch her hips sway, her pink hair bobbing as she leaves.

I do it anyway.

"My number looks good on her," Miles says, slinging an arm around my neck.

The women head down the hall together, Nova squeezing her fist.

Mine looks better.

6

NOVA

"It's too sweet." Mari makes a face.

"It's cake. Is there such a thing?" My fork glides through the smooth cake, and I pop a bite into my mouth. The soft lemon flavor makes me moan.

"I want to try the lavender buttercream again."

It's my third day in Denver and officially the weekend. We're testing wedding cakes at a fancy bakery in town.

All three we've tried, including a chocolate hazelnut with vanilla frosting, have been delicious. But Mari can't seem to find one she likes.

"It's better than sex, right?" A woman around my age blows in, her golden skin flawless and her dark hair twisted back in dozens of tiny braids. "Chloe sends her half-assed apologies. She got sucked into a meeting, so I get to play taste-tester with you. Which is lucky for you because I have better taste." Her dancing eyes land on me. "I'm Brooke. You must be Nova."

She folds me in a hug that's warm.

"You're biased," Mari points out. "You found the baker."

"They hired me to help them with their social media presence. I knew they'd be perfect for the wedding," she explains as she drops onto a stool next to me.

"Do you work with the team, too?"

"They wish. I have my own empire."

"She means her million Instagram followers," Mari supplies.

"Almost two, and I busted my ass for every one of them." Brooke winks. "But my brother, Jayden, plays point guard."

A basketball team is only a handful of people in an entire city. How the hell is everyone connected to this one?

She takes a bite, but my mind drifts back to my visit to the stadium yesterday and the man I encountered in the gym.

A tall, tattooed god glistening with sweat, his eyes burning like coals.

On the plane, he was impressive but down to earth.

But the stadium was his natural environment.

When I got back in the car, I yanked out my phone and typed "Kodiaks basketball players" into the search bar.

Milliseconds later, I had my answer.

Clayton Wade.

Power forward.

Twenty-nine years old.

Two-time all-star.

Six feet, five grumpy inches of athlete wrapped in a "fuck you" tattoo.

My dream guy wasn't some stranger I'd never see again that I could safely fantasize about.

He's Harlan's star player.

"You should play basketball. I bet you'd be good at it."

He must have thought I was such an idiot.

Except the way he looked at me made me feel as if I was burning up.

I scroll through images of him dunking the ball, running up the court.

In interviews.

In media campaigns.

In one image, he's looking straight at the camera. He's impossibly gorgeous and grumpy, as if the idea of standing still for a single photo puts an irreversible kink in his day.

And I told him all my secrets.

"I owe you a tattoo."

"This is how you redeem it."

The best thing to do would be forget we ever met.

It's why after returning from the stadium, I tried to scrub the number from my hand.

Clay wrote it in Sharpie.

Two days later, it's starting to fade, but I still keep my hand clenched tight when I'm around Mari.

"Nova has a boyfriend. He's perfect. We spent time with him at Christmas."

I snap back to the present.

"Oh?" Brooke says.

"I keep telling her she needs to get him to propose."

"No pressure," Brooke weighs in, misunderstanding my silence. "I don't even know if I want to get married. Of course, my parents would love it. But I'm twenty-three. I have at least another ten years before I need to figure anything out. If they want grandchildren, they'll wait for Jay to provide them."

"Do players date?" I ask, relieved for the change of subject. "It sounds like they're on the road all the time and it would be hard to keep a relationship going."

Brooke shifts on her seat. "You don't know?"

"Know what?"

"My brother and Chloe."

My eyes widen, but my sister nods.

"They had a thing back in college," Brooke says. "Neither of them will say who dumped who, but I still give him shit about it."

Wow. A breakup is hard enough, but seeing the person you loved every single day would be so much worse, especially if there were unresolved feelings.

Brooke spears a bite of another cake. It falls off her fork, misses the table and hits the floor. "Whoops."

Mari looks offended, but Brooke only shrugs.

"We've done way worse." I stab another bite of cake, holding it in my fork in a catapult position directed at my sister. "Remember when we used to have food fights?"

"Outside, when we were ten. Don't you dare," Mari hisses.

Brooke laughs.

My grip slips and the cake shoots toward Mari, landing in a plop in front of her. My sister jumps from her seat, emitting a screech as she wipes delicately at her dark sweater.

"There's no way I got you."

"There're a spot of lemon right here." She points at an invisible dot on her sleeve.

"Well, if it causes you so much stress, you should probably get the lavender."

Brooke tosses her head back and laughs.

~

As I'm leaving the bathroom after a shower, I find Mari next to my closet.

"Hey, Mar? What are you doing?"

She straightens, holding up something in her fingers. "I was looking to see if you had that bracelet of Mom's. I was thinking I might wear it for the wedding."

"Oh. Um, it's not in there."

"What is this?" She lifts something from the jewelry box.

The quarter-carat diamond ring glints in the light.

She gasps. "Nova! You and Brad?! Who else knows?"

A lump rises in my throat.

I can't tell her it's the one thing of any value he didn't take—and only because it was on my finger and that would've made it hard to escape without a trace.

But she's so excited, and for once, I can't find the words.

"We should call him!" she goes on when I don't answer.

"*No!*"

Mari's eyes widen.

I think she's going to press the matter, but instead, understanding dawns on her face.

"Because it's my wedding and you don't want to

pull focus." She draws me into a hug. "I know I give you a hard time, but once in a while, you do something grown up like this."

The truth is on the tip of my tongue, but I don't want to disappoint my sister and make her think I can't do anything right.

She leaves, and I drop onto the bed.

Harlan and Mari have been nothing but welcoming. Still, keeping this secret is a weight on my chest that's growing each day. I feel claustrophobic in this huge house.

I need to do something wild.

To get out of here.

I set the ring back in the jewelry box.

There's no one I can talk to about this. No one who understands the pressure I'm under and who wouldn't judge me for what I'm doing.

Except one person.

Clayton Wade might be a superstar, but he also knows my damage.

And he never looked as if he judged me.

With a glance back at the empty doorway, I open my hand and stare at the ten-digit number on it.

I shouldn't. I'm trying to sort out my life.

Fantasizing about the most famous athlete on my future BIL's NBA team is not the way to do that.

I bite my cheek and reach for my phone.

My fingers punch in the digits from my palm, and I type out a message.

Delete.
Another one.
Delete.
I try one more time.
Then take a breath and hit Send.

7

CLAY

"You're late," Miles tells Rookie as he comes in the door.

"I dropped Wade's laundry off in the wrong place."

Hollers echo off the aging walls as Rookie slides into the booth with a grin.

Mile High feels as close to home as anywhere. In contrast to some of the shiny new spots, this one has history. Old oak booths, faded paint, dull gold taps, and smiling faces. It's the team's unofficial brewery.

"Clay, can I get you another beer?" the waitress asks. The service here is already good, but she's extra attentive to me over the other guys.

I shake my head.

Earlier this year, I loaned money to the owner, who was struggling to make rent after the landlord jacked the prices after thirty years—on the condition he kept it between us. Don't want anyone thinking I'm a bleeding heart.

In fact, it's easier if I have a reputation for being difficult because it keeps people from messing with me—in the game and in life.

It's been a long day. Between practice, watching tape, and a sponsor engagement, I haven't had a minute to relax.

But it's getting near the season.

People have this idea athletes can eat anything they want, but the opposite is true. You want to be competitive in this league for a long time, you have to pay attention to the details.

"Why do you put up with running his errands, Rookie?" Miles tosses after the waitress departs.

"There another option?"

The other guys laugh.

It's normal for rookies to pull some chores first year. Everyone just assumed he'd be my rookie because our games are the most similar style. Plus, I'm the biggest star, and he's arguably the future.

Playing with me will set him up for a pro career. Rookie wants to watch me, listen to me, learn from me. Hoping some of the shine will rub off on him.

Thing is, I never signed on to be a mentor. I've got enough of my own shit to handle.

"You think scoring will be easy because I'm here?" I drawl.

"Hell yeah. You'll be pulling all the defenses," Rookie tosses back.

"Which gives you touches. But you gotta make 'em," I point out. "Put the work in so when the ball's in your hands, you can do your job. And next year, if you survive that long, you won't be the new kid. They'll have you scouted up to here." I lift a hand. "Then I can't protect you."

The first year of my rookie season, I started every game, was an all-star at twenty-one.

I got any shot I wanted, on or off the court.

More than that, I adapted. Sophomore slump is a real thing, but I worked harder on my game, my body, my head than anyone else and came out stronger.

Fast forward seven years of more or less smooth sailing—at least as much as they can be in the NBA.

I was put on this earth to play basketball, but last year, I got a rude reminder of how fragile this can all be.

I'm not about to tap out, or step back, or let anyone ruin my shot.

A text comes through from my agent.

I'm working on some options for the start of the season. We're keeping it discreet like you asked.

I exhale hard.

Never thought of myself as someone who keeps

secrets. But lately, I leave out a lot more than I say. Even with Jay, the guy who's the closest thing I have to a best friend.

These guys are my team, but they don't get what I've been through.

They don't know what it's like to stare down the barrel of your career, your future, and know how close you came to it all being over.

The smallest misstep and it *will* be over.

This Kodiaks team will be better than last year. Top eight in the West, maybe top six if Rookie delivers and my body holds up to the grind of the season.

But there's a big difference between sixth in the West and first in the league.

If I want to make it to the top of the mountain, I might not have a lot of years to do it.

A group of women walk by, sneaking looks at us and giggling.

They're objectively attractive, but I can't bring myself to care.

It's been two days since I left the number on Nova's hand.

I haven't heard a sound from her. Forty-eight hours of practice and life and not a damned peep.

The way she looked at me in the bathroom of that plane, like she fucking saw me, was addictive.

Maybe I misread.

The fact that most women in this town would let

me buy them a drink—and a healthy number of those would wait in the bathroom with open legs—doesn't soothe my ego.

They're not her.

Forget it. What were you going to do with Harlan's sister-in-law anyway?

As if on command, my phone buzzes.

Unknown number: Hey, it's Nova. I hope this is the right number, or I'm going to feel like an idiot.

Her pretty face in my mind wipes away my tortured thoughts.

I type back.

Clay: Who are you looking for?

Unknown number: Tall. Grumpy. Writes on people with permanent marker.

I reach for a water in the center of the table and down it.

Clay: Doesn't sound like me.

Miles cracks up at something Jay said. Atlas's shoulders rock so hard the table shakes.

Unknown number: I want my tattoo.

They're only words, but they send a surge of adrenaline through me.

I shouldn't say yes. She's Harlan's family, or practically, which means I can't trust her. Plus, Jay's right that I need to focus on my game and not get distracted by a pretty face.

But she's a lifeline.

I'm surrounded by my guys, but I feel alone.

Clay: I'm coming.

I pocket the phone.

"Wait, where you going?" Miles calls as I shift out of the booth.

"Out."

I signal the waitress to tell her to put the team's drinks on my tab, then I head out of the bar without a backward glance.

8

CLAY

*S*he told me to park on the road.
Evidently the list of things I'll do to get under Harlan's skin won't include showing up at his door to take out his future sister-in-law tonight.

Most of the fancy communities around here are gated, but this one isn't. I pull up at the foot of the driveway and send a text to let her know I'm here. I cut the engine but leave the radio on, turning over what happened earlier at the bar.

I want to win—I have to—and this team isn't my ticket to a championship. Harlan won't admit it, but he's not stupid. He knows it, too.

The passenger door opens, and Nova shifts inside in a blur of pink.

"Going down the drainpipe looks way easier in movies," she pants.

She's silhouetted by the interior lights. Her black

yoga pants and long-sleeved shirt hug her curves and give cat burglar vibes. "Seriously?"

"No. I snuck out the back."

Then with a click of her door, we're in darkness again.

Her scent is light and a little smoky, like some desert flower, and I resist the temptation to lean over and inhale.

I start the engine and pull into the street.

"Cute car. Electric." She runs her hand over the dash. "I didn't realize these were available yet."

"They're not."

"But they are for Clayton Wade."

She's teasing me.

"I get what I want. On and off the court."

She laughs. "Wow. What is that, like a line?"

"No. It's the truth."

"If you really get everything you want, you should look happier."

I cut a look over at her, but she's all shadows.

"Enough about me. Tell me about the tattoo you're getting."

"I want a big one."

"I see."

"Huge. Angry." She spits out the words.

"Angry what?"

"An animal. A cougar, or a bear, or a lion. Something that will tell people I'm feral and there's no point getting close to me." She turns toward me. "Are you laughing?"

"A little."

"I didn't know you laughed."

"Once a day. You're lucky I didn't hit my quota yet."

"Must've been a rough day."

"I guess," I admit. "You?"

"Same."

Traffic is sparse at this time of night.

We drive in silence a minute, but it's lighter than before.

"Do you ever feel like the walls are closing in?" she asks. "As if every time you enter a room, it's smaller than the last time, but no one notices but you?"

My hands clench the steering wheel as I think of the pressure from the guys, the fans, myself. "Every day."

The plan was to take her for the tattoo, watch her from a safe distance, and figure out what it is about her that I can't kick from my head.

Getting a tattoo in a dark moment can be a reminder, but I don't want her doing something she'll regret.

I pull a U-turn and go south, heading out of town.

"This is the way to the tattoo parlor?" she asks as the buildings thin out.

"No."

"You said you'd take me." Nova straightens in her seat.

"I said I'd pick you up. Never said where we were going. You still want one in an hour, we'll do it," I say.

She groans and slumps back in her seat. For the next minute, she stares out the window.

"You don't look worried about where we are going," I note. "I could be kidnapping you."

"Promise?"

Her hopeful voice starts a tightening deep in my gut.

Suddenly I'm picturing exactly that. Taking her far from this town. Not looking back.

When we get to our destination, I find parking at a lot off the road. There's almost no one here except campers.

"Red Rocks?" Nova shifts out of the car and tilts up her face. "Wow, this place is unreal. It feels like you're close to heaven, or space, or both."

"That's the altitude talking."

"I've heard they have the most epic concerts and music festivals. You must come all the time."

"Never," I admit.

"How long have you been here?"

I do the math. "Eight months."

"So, you don't like music."

"I like it fine. I just don't have time."

"That sounds awful."

"Awful?" I scoff. "You know how many people want to be me?"

She cocks her head. "Lonely, then. Because no matter how many people want to be you, you're the only one who is."

Nova heads off toward the amphitheatre before I can respond.

To the Kodiaks, I'm an asset.

To the fans, I'm a fantasy.

To Rookie and the kids coming up, I'm a god.

It's been a long time since anyone talked to me like I'm a person.

I pull my hoodie up around my head on the off chance we run into anyone, but it's quiet.

She scrambles over the dusty ridges, laughing.

Nova is warm and alive. She's like a baby animal running around.

I wonder, when was the last time I was that vibrant?

"Careful," I warn her.

"I wore running shoes."

I stare a little too long at her legs. "Those are sandals."

"They're sport sandals."

"Not a thing."

"Okay, footwear police." She ignores me and keeps running along the rows of rock. "It feels better out here. Like I'm not trapped. Like I can be exactly who I want."

I follow her, my long strides keeping up with her without effort. "Who's that?"

"Someone who can take care of herself instead of needing my sister to do it for me."

I think of my own sister, how when she was in the hospital as a teen, I went deeper into my basketball, unable to handle what I couldn't control.

"Actually, it's not even that. The thing she likes most about me is my fiancé."

Every muscle in me tenses. "I thought you said you were single."

"No. Yes," she amends.

I leap forward, cutting off her path. "How the fuck can you not know if you're engaged?"

A lot of people think athletes are into cheating, but I'm not. Even the idea of it makes me seethe.

I mean what I told Jay, that I'm not looking for a distraction, but I hate thinking she might be someone else's to stare at out of the corner of their eye.

To write their number on.

To wonder what it is about her that makes the air change when she's near.

Nova shrugs, looking small and younger than before.

"He left without saying goodbye. But technically I didn't have a chance to give him the ring back, so..."

My anger shifts targets to whatever prick hurt her.

"He was an asshole."

She wraps her arms around her, the breeze blowing her hair. "Maybe I'm the asshole. He was successful and independent. He said all the right things. Mari liked him."

"You're not the asshole."

"How do you know?"

"Just do."

Her lips curve in the dark. Her breathing is steady and even.

"My parents used to say I had the worst taste in guys. But they died in a plane crash three years ago."

She says it matter-of-factly, like she's telling me the weather or her favorite color.

Nova shifts past me to start scaling the rows of seats again.

It bothers me that she has no one. No parents, no boyfriend, a sister she's on strained terms with.

Doesn't mean she's yours.

A dozen yards ahead, she slips, her hands breaking her fall. I hear her sharp intake of breath and the hitch that tells me she's hurt.

Shit.

I quickly scale the seats between us, then sit on the dirt next to her. I push up her sleeve to feel her wrist with my fingers, each joint and tendon. There's nothing seriously out of place, but a little whimper escapes her when I press harder.

"Sorry," I mutter, not sure whether I mean for hurting her or for everyone else who has. "Ice it when you get home unless you want it to blow up on you by morning."

"Thanks." Nova leans back until her back kisses the dirt, cradling her arm across her chest.

I'm memorizing every line of her silhouette, the feel of her breath light on my skin.

"I bet you never get caught up in your own head," she says. "Never question yourself. Girls would probably sell their left tit to date you."

"Sucks because the left is my favorite."

Her laugh is warm and bright.

I can't remember the last time I talked this much to anyone. About anything real, anyway.

"They want me for what I represent," I hear myself say. "They have some idea of what it would be like to be with me or to be seen with me. They don't give a shit about *me*."

"You must have had a real relationship?" she asks.

"I'm on the road half the year. It doesn't fit with my lifestyle."

"I bet the right girl would bend over backward to fit with your lifestyle. She'd know your stat sheet and whether you like smooth or crunchy peanut butter."

My lips twitch in the dark. "That's not in my official bio."

This time her laughter is lower, stroking along my spine.

"I like crunchy peanut butter. Now you know something they don't."

Her smile widens, and I want to frame it.

"You like being famous, but you like being anonymous more. That's why you didn't tell me who you were on the plane."

I'm not sure how I feel about her analyzing me. For now, I let it slide.

"When people know who you are, they expect things of you. It was nice to meet someone who didn't expect anything."

She turns that over. "What do *you* want?"

"To be the best. Like Jordan or Kobe." I've said as much in public.

My family gave up lots to help me be that. My parents came to all my games, even though it took us away from my sister.

"Are you?"

"I was on track. All-star. All-league. My stats were only matched by three guys in history, all of whom were Finals MVPs. But I haven't won a championship. Until I get that ring, there's still a mountain to climb." I flex my knee. "Took a trade here, thinking we'd have a shot to go all the way. Then I tore my ACL. All of it came crashing down. Surgery last year. Months of rehab."

Now, all that's left are questions. Ones I confidently answer in public but can't stop asking myself in private.

"But you're better now. You can help Denver win," she presses.

That's what I'm telling everyone.

I won't tell her my plans to leave. She'd tell Harlan, and tipping him off now would cause problems. It's fine if he thinks I'm disgruntled, but I don't want him knowing we're actively looking for an out before my agent and I have the right buyer lined up. He could try to move me somewhere I don't want, or worse—try to keep me here just to prove a point.

A rustling sound has us both jumping.

"What is that?" she demands.

"Cougars. Or bears. You know, those angry animals you wanted tattooed on you."

It's a joke, but it seems less funny now.

She shivers.

I reach an arm around her, shielding her body with mine.

We're lined up everywhere. There's no skin-to-skin contact, but I can feel her heat through our clothes.

"I'm sure they're just protecting their own," she whispers.

So am I.

My grip on her tightens.

My ears strain to hear anything in the distance, but mostly I'm dialed into her.

Her scent. Her heartbeat. The feel of her in my arms. I swallow the groan as she shifts against me.

Her hand brushes my abs where my shirt has ridden up. The pull I feel deepens into an ache.

"Nova."

She tilts her head in the dark, the only indication she heard me.

"How'd you find out your fiancé left?"

"A note in the mailbox the same day as Mari's wedding invitation." Her usually bright voice is soft and reflective. "He said our life wasn't what he wanted, that I wasn't what he wanted. I found out later he took our joint savings and stole from the company we both worked at. I've been on probation from work while they investigate."

Fuck.

That had to hurt like hell, and she's trying to stand on her own feet.

I'm a king with no room at my side for a queen. Hanging with me will only mess with her plans.

If I want to protect her, I have to tamp down on this attraction.

I pull back and scan the horizon for any signs of wildlife.

"Come on. I'm taking you home."

9

NOVA

"You fall asleep on me?" Clay asks as we turn in to Country Hills.

"Maybe."

The entire drive home, I was aware of him filling the car with his big body and even bigger presence.

"Don't make me carry you back up the drainpipe," he drawls.

I laugh in the dark, my wrist throbbing dully in time with the bass from the speakers.

The pain is an afterthought.

Tonight, I ran through Red Rocks with the baddest guy in basketball, and I felt like a wild girl.

With him, I don't have to pretend. Confessing what I've been holding in felt freeing.

Clay's different than anyone I've met. I liked getting to know more about him and sensed he doesn't talk to many people. For a man who lives his life in the spotlight, he's so private.

"I'm sure you could carry me before your knee problems."

"I could carry you now. You're a hell of a lot lighter than what I lift."

His gruff response thrills me.

I'm thrown back to when I was nestled between his legs, my hand on his chest through the thin T-shirt under his sweatshirt.

I didn't realize how long it's been since I was with a guy, not to mention since I was touched or held in a way that made me feel alive.

He must know the effect he has on me, but I want to believe it's not one-way. For a moment in the dark, I could have sworn he wanted me, too.

His phone lights up on the console between us.

"Someone's texting you…"

My voice trails off as I see the flesh-colored image.

It's a woman.

Naked, or nearly, with a Kardashian figure and barely-there lingerie over huge breasts and a very waxed everything else.

"Sorry, I wasn't trying to look," I say, embarrassed.

Clay glances at the screen, his expression revealing nothing.

He flips the phone facedown.

This is probably normal for him. We're from different worlds. He could have any woman he wants—glamorous, confident. I forgot it for a minute, but this is a blunt reminder.

We drive the rest of the way in silence.

"Don't turn up the driveway," I tell him when we reach the house.

Clay stops at the foot of the driveway, and I reach for my seatbelt, pressing the release button.

It doesn't give.

I try again.

Over and over, until I'm slamming it with my finger.

"Dammit." I slump against my seat, feeling the warmth emanating from his body as he leans in.

"What's wrong?" he demands.

He means now, in this car, but my head is still back at the park.

"When you said you were going to take me home, for a moment I imagined you meant with you."

He stills over me.

We spent the last two hours talking under the stars, until the moment we heard those wild animals.

Instantly, he shuttered. The walls went up, the man I was with vanished like a ghost.

Clay pumped some intoxicating drug through my system, and now that I'm back for more, he's nowhere to be found.

"Maybe it's crazy to imagine you wanting to, but

for a second..." I huff out a breath as I cradle my wrist. "It didn't feel crazy."

I half expect him to laugh, thinking of the picture message and the stunning woman praying for the slightest show of interest from the all-star next to me.

He doesn't laugh.

He bends closer, the scent of wood and ash mingling into a heady aroma.

"I don't do that, Nova."

The blood pounds between my thighs, echoing the throbbing in my wrist.

"You don't have sex," I counter.

I swear I hear his teeth grind.

"Not the way you'd want to."

"How do you know what I'd want?"

"You're coming off a breakup," he goes on, ignoring my question. "You should be handled with care."

My head falls back in a helpless gesture. "Honestly? I just want to be handled."

I'm in Denver for my sister, to prove that I have my life together—not to throw myself at a basketball star who's probably visited more vaginas than cities.

But all I can think about since the plane ride is how horny I am. I'm aching for pleasure and connection.

The radio's still on, playing an old Drake song. I want to reach for the dashboard and turn it up until it vibrates through every inch of me.

"Do you have Miles' number?" My voice is steady. "Because I kind of thought we had a vibe in the kitchen and—"

"You're not dating Miles," Clay interrupts sharply.

"I never said date." I let that settle between us. "Maybe he'll take me to get my tattoo."

Clay's gaze drops to my mouth, lingering.

"Nova."

My name is a warning, for him or me, I'm not sure. His hands are a weight against my hip, his warmth permeating my clothes.

"What?"

The drumming of my heart picks up. The air between us crackles with electricity, pulling us closer.

"Don't pout," he rasps, his voice the ominous roll of thunder. "I'm selfish enough to give you what you think you want."

My heart skips.

What I want? What about what he wants?

Because the tight line of his jaw says he's fighting himself.

We're a breath apart, close enough to feel each other's warmth. His woodsy scent fills my nostrils with a heady, dizzying aroma.

I'm a bound sacrifice tied up in front of a sexy monster. One that's looking at me as though he can't decide whether I'm entertaining or maddening.

I should be nowhere near this man, and yet here I

am in a car with him, feeling strangely empowered by his presence.

"You're right," I whisper. "If I'm going to make a mistake tonight, better to make one that doesn't leave a mark."

I reach up to brush my lips across his.

At the first touch of our skin, a shiver of desire floods me, zinging through my breasts, my stomach, and all the way down to my thighs.

Clay's mouth is softer than I expect. His closeness is a drug all its own.

He doesn't kiss me back, but doesn't pull away either. He's a rock wall, firm and unyielding.

It's an act. It has to be.

Even if he isn't starved for me like I am for him, he's attracted. Curious.

The music pulses and throbs around us.

My skin is ablaze everywhere we're touching. I cling to him, as if he's the one to put out the flames instead of the one to start the fire.

I kiss him the way I want to, not the way I think I should. Not the way the woman in the picture would kiss him, but the way I wanted to kiss the man who protected me in the dark with his body.

The one who doesn't see that he deserves protection, too.

I reach up to thread my fingers through his hair and tug. When I exhale a trembling breath, his lips part.

I change the angle and let out a little sigh that's lost in his mouth before forcing myself to pull back.

Clay's half-lowered lids brush my cheeks.

"The fuck was that?" he murmurs.

My heart hammers in my chest. I can't meet his eyes. "I wanted to know what it would feel like if you kissed me."

He curses again.

I start to reach for my seatbelt, but his arms are a cage.

He grabs my chin and forces my gaze up. His eyes are glittering gems in the dark.

"That wasn't it."

Before I can react, his mouth slams down on mine.

He's as rough as I was gentle.

His lips and tongue wreak havoc with my mouth, exploring every inch of me.

My pulse skyrockets as he tugs my earlobe between his teeth.

My body throbs, every nerve ending coming alive under his touch.

I can't breathe. I don't want to. I need more of this, of him.

If he's trying to scare me away, it's not working.

He strokes down my sides, one huge hand cupping my breast. My body swells, my nipples hardening and begging for his touch.

I arch toward him, my hand slipping beneath his shirt to land on smooth, muscled abs.

Clay groans his approval low in his throat, sending a delicious thrill coursing through me.

His thumb presses against my hip.

I reach around his waist, imagine the dark tattooed lines writhing beneath my —

Click.

The next second, his warmth is gone, and so is my seatbelt. He's back on his side of the car, and the space between us is a chasm.

"Goodnight, Nova."

Clay stares out the windshield, not meeting my eyes.

I brush my lips with a finger to make sure they're still there.

I wait for him to say something else. Anything else.

He doesn't.

My limbs are still heavy, but I force myself to move.

I grab the door handle and launch myself out, slamming it after me before I remember I'm trying to be quiet.

I sprint up the driveway without looking back. I'm halfway to the house before I notice the throbbing in my wrist start up again.

That moment of exercising my own power *was* a

bad idea. Not because I touched the baddest guy in basketball, my brother-in-law's troublemaking all-star, all while my sister thinks I'm engaged to someone else.

No, it's because instead of being like every girl who wants to kiss Clayton Wade, I've moved into the slightly smaller pool of every girl he's kissed who wants more.

10

NOVA

Sleeping is hard. I toss and turn, agitated and hot.

I'm still cursing Clay the next morning.

He barely touched me, and I caught fire.

He was as cool as ever afterward, as if we shared dessert recipes last night instead of a scorching-hot kiss.

Even though I tried to shove him from my mind and my fantasies, he's been the star ever since I met his gorgeous, grumpy ass.

So, this morning in the shower, I pictured him on his knees, begging me to forgive him for the mixed messages.

Last night wasn't a date. He made it clear that he's not looking for that.

Except every time we were close, he had zero problem staring.

Grumpy Baller: How's the wrist?

The text came through when I got out of the shower. I named his contact that after I arrived home last night.

Another message followed half an hour later that was only two question marks. He probably expected me to jump at hearing from him.

I didn't reply. I've got other things to do today than join the millions of people lining up for a glance from Clayton Wade.

"Nova?"

I look up from my borrowed car to find Harlan in the doorway of the garage, dressed impeccably in a dark suit and silk tie.

"Everything okay? I'm off to meet Mari and Chloe for a dress fitting."

"Yes, I don't want to keep you." But he doesn't move, and I wait him out. "The past few months, I've been focused on the team, and when the season starts, it'll only get more intense. That's why I want to give Mari a wedding she'll never forget."

I lean a hip against the car door. "It will be."

"I want to surprise Mari with a gift. A new philanthropic program in her name to help kids with challenging upbringings find passions they can turn into careers. Do you think she'll like it?"

My heart melts at his thoughtfulness and generosity. "She'll love it."

"Good. It's becoming more of an undertaking than I thought, but I don't want to let her in on the secret. In a way, I blame myself for wanting to move ahead with this wedding instead of waiting. But after she was passed over for that promotion last spring, she's been working harder than ever, and if she gets promoted now, I'm afraid she'll never take time off."

My smile falters as I remember when I got kicked out of my apartment for falling behind on rent last year. The job I was working at the time, the one before the agency, didn't pay me for two months. They kept saying it was coming, but they went bankrupt first.

When my sister called and found out, she insisted on flying to Boston to help me fix it. She was dealing with extra projects at work but didn't say anything about the promotion.

Harlan goes on, oblivious. "I was hoping to get your input on what I've put together. Not from a programming perspective, just quick reactions and if there are any opportunities I've missed that might have special meaning for Mari. I'd also like to consult with Robin, who runs our children's camp for the Kodiak Foundation, but I haven't had a moment."

I don't want to be something Mari has to fix. I want to help *her*.

The MOH job might be taken, but I can do this.

"Let me help."

His brows lift in surprise. "Are you sure? You're doing more than enough."

"Nonsense. I'd be happy to take a look, and I can also run it by Robin if you send me an introduction."

He nods, looking as if a weight has been lifted from his tailored shoulders. "Mari's lucky to have you."

Pleasure courses through me.

"Maybe you could send pictures from the fitting?" he goes on.

"Don't press your luck," I call as I shift into the Volvo.

∼

"What're you drawing?"

Brooke's voice makes my head snap up, and I cover my sketchbook.

She tugs it out of my fingers and her mouth drops open. Her dark eyes sparkle with delight. "This is really good. You're an artist."

"Thanks. I need more source material to finish it."

Brooke's lips curve. "I bet."

This morning, I pulled out the sketchpad I haven't used since I arrived in Denver and started drawing.

Back in art school, we'd start with a project in

mind, an intention. Today, I let myself draw whatever came to me.

Guess I shouldn't have been surprised by the result.

The guy is up over a basketball rim, dunking. I haven't started to add the tattoos, so there's no way she can tell it's Clay—I hope.

But having the pencils and paper in my hands again feels right. Even before this trip, I hadn't drawn since Brad left. Maybe for a while before, actually.

Art has always been my way of connecting with the world. Now, it's as if I'm picking up the phone and dialing a friend I haven't spoken to in too long.

"Nova, you're up." Mari looks over from where she's inspecting the fit of Chloe's dress.

Chloe stands on the pedestal, looking stunning in a soft-pink gown that sets off her skin and dark hair.

"What're you doing?" Mari asks.

"She's daydreaming," Brooke drawls, shooting me a little smile as she passes back the sketchbook.

I tuck it into my purse and get ready to try on my bridesmaid's dress.

"I wish you'd do your hair a natural color," Mari says as I slip into the dress.

"Hot pink is found in nature. There are anemones that are exactly this shade." I try to reach around but can't find the zipper. "Can you—"

"I've got it."

She zips me up the back, and I smile in thanks. Then I take in my reflection.

Brooke makes a catcall. "Nova, you look hot."

I smooth my hands down the satin.

"I wouldn't change a thing," the seamstress says. "It was made for you."

"Even with the hair?" I tease, and Mari rolls her eyes.

"Don't push it."

It feels like a girl squad moment. We're bonding, and it's good.

"Hey, Nova. Is this the design firm you work at?" Chloe holds up her phone.

I finish changing out of the dress and back into my street clothes before glancing over. "Yeah. Why?"

"Mari said there was a nice picture of you and your boyfriend since she hasn't seen any pics lately."

My stomach tightens. "Oh. They might have taken it down."

She clicks around on her screen, then frowns. "You're not listed on the staff page. Neither is he."

The pain in my chest is my heart thudding against my ribs.

I cross to Chloe, the fabric of the dress sliding over my skin, and look over her shoulder. They've deleted me from the page altogether.

"Nova?" Mari asks. There's a note of dread in her voice, and it makes me feel worse.

I don't want to do this here, in front of everyone, but they're all looking at me.

"I'm on leave from work," I say.

Mari inhales sharply. "And Brad?"

I shake my head. "He's gone."

"From the firm?"

"From everywhere. I haven't seen him in two months."

Three pairs of shocked eyes lock on me.

Mari's mouth works. She sinks onto the chaise, blinking. "You lost your job?"

"I didn't lose it. They put me on leave pending an investigation."

"What did you do, Nova?"

A ball of shame rises up my throat, and the backs of my eyes burn. "I don't... I can't."

I turn and run for the door.

∽

At a coffee shop a few blocks away, I order a cappuccino to soothe my stomach.

When it comes to Mari, I always feel like a little kid. She has her shit figured out, and I'm the joke.

I was trying to avoid talking about Brad and work, but by keeping it from her, it's made things worse.

Even though I can't hide out forever, right now I need the space. I pull open my sketchbook and pick up drawing where I left off.

My cell rings a few minutes in.

It's not Mari.

Grumpy Baller calling.

I don't feel like talking to him, but can't bring myself to hit decline.

"You didn't answer my text," Clay says without waiting for a hello.

"And the state of my wrist was a national emergency?"

"Is it?"

I roll my wrist around. "No."

I did ice it, and the treatment did help.

"Tell me what's so important you didn't text me back," he says.

I groan. "Are you this bossy with your teammates?"

"I'm charmingly persistent."

"Debatable." But I take a breath and fill him in, feeling as though I'm confessing and burdening him way too much.

He listens, his silence punctuated with steady breathing.

"It was humiliating," I finish. "I felt like I was ten all over again and she won the spelling bee and I didn't make it past the second word—*catastrophe*. I carried around her trophy though."

"That's decent."

I squeeze my eyes shut. "And pretended it was mine."

There's a sound like a half laugh, half grunt. "Can't see how it's your sister's business what you do. Who you date or where you work, either."

The tight ball in my chest eases a bit. "We used to tell each other everything. I'm not sure when that changed."

"You have to follow your own path. Everyone I went to school with wanted to be a doctor or a lawyer. Deciding to pursue basketball wasn't the easy choice—it was the hard one."

"It sounds lonely."

"Sometimes being different is."

My attention falls to my drawing. As ego-bruised as I am from last night, I'm not ready to hang up.

"Do you know anything about children's charitable foundations?"

"Ask Chloe. The team's foundation is part of her portfolio."

I bite my lip. "I don't want to involve her."

I tell him I'm trying to learn to help out a friend but don't admit it's for Harlan. From what my future brother-in-law said, he and Clay don't have the best relationship. Solving that is definitely beyond the scope of my powers, and at this point, I suspect that even asking about it would get me shut down fast.

"I've done some work with the foundation. I could answer your questions," Clay says when I'm finished.

I'm surprised, both because I didn't see anything

in his profile about that and because he's offering. "You kicked me out of your car last night, and now you're offering to help."

"I needed my beauty sleep."

"Shouldn't that be my line?"

There's a pause.

"You get any prettier, it's gonna be a problem."

My heart skips.

A compliment from Clayton Wade? It's like a diamond pried from the dirt.

That—and the safety of being miles away from him—makes me bold.

"I thought you might have had to get to other company. Like the Kardashian who texted you."

"Huh?"

I wave a hand in the air. "Or whatever you call your hot-girl Kodiak groupies. Kodashians?"

He snorts. It feels good to have a joke with him.

"That's it, your laugh for the day," I point out.

"Right."

"Unless maybe the photo didn't include her left boob, so it was a no?"

This time, he chuckles out loud. "That would be a dealbreaker."

"Oh no, that's two laughs," I warn. "A clear violation of the one-a-day rule."

"Guess you're my exception."

I like the sound of that.

I survey the drawing in front of me again, glad he can't see it.

"Good, because I'm not lining up like one of your Kodashians."

"Never asked you to."

"And I don't care who you got off with last night," I inform him, cradling the phone between my shoulder and ear as I start to add the tattoos on his shoulder.

His biceps are bigger, I'm sure of it.

I bite my lip and shade the contour accordingly.

"Then I don't need to tell you it was a solo mission."

My pencil bounces off my knee, clattering to the floor.

I uncross and recross my legs, feeling a delicious tug between my thighs as I imagine him lying back in bed, reaching into his sweatpants and wrapping his fist around his length.

Last night, he made it seem like he regretted the kiss. Today, he's planting the image of him getting himself off squarely in my mind.

Someone hollers his name in the background.

I glance at the clock and realize we've been talking for fifteen minutes. "Are you in practice?"

"Yeah. I should go before Coach fines me."

"He can do that?! Holy. Hurry and hang up."

"I will."

But I'm touched he ducked out to talk to me.

"Wait! Say hi to Miles for me," I say as I bend to retrieve my pencil.

I'm rewarded with a huff. "The fuck is it with you and Miles?"

My grin widens. "We're destined."

When he answers, it's a low rumble I feel as though he's pressed his lips to my skin.

"Wasn't Miles you were clinging to last night."

My core throbs.

I'm still tingling when he clicks off.

When I go back to my drawing, it turns out I *can* finish him from memory.

11

CLAY

"First preseason game is in two days. Set your feet on defence, look for your teammates, and let's get a win," Coach hollers after blowing the whistle.

Rookie takes his shots and makes them. The other guys cheer him on, and he grins.

I step up and do the same.

I've been doubling up on my gym time, plus ice baths every night, since I got back.

Recovery's a bitch, and I'm bending over.

I feel the anticipation heading into the preseason. Even if my future is up in the air, the competitive drive is kicking in.

After practice, Coach gathers us around. "We're seeing some good progress individually, but we won't know how that stacks up until we start playing games.

Now, I hope you gentlemen have been practicing your singing."

"Singing?" Rookie looks around.

Jayden laughs. "It's a preseason tradition."

Groans go up, but everyone starts singing the team's unofficial anthem.

I snort as eyes land on me.

"You avoided it last year by being new. Now you're a vet," Jay chides.

"I can't interrupt your masterpiece," I toss back.

Coach's eyes land on me. "You got a problem, Wade?"

I wasn't looking to pick a fight today.

Or maybe I am.

I'm on edge today, have been all week.

"Singing doesn't help us win basketball games."

"It does around here."

We stare each other down.

Normally, I don't have a problem with Coach, but I don't have time for dumb traditions when I'm doing everything in my power to be the guy who can win basketball games again.

"Clay." Chloe's standing along the sidelines, a tablet in her hand. "Harlan wants a word."

"Only one?" I towel off and head that way. But the truth is, I'm relieved by the interruption.

Harlan's lurking in the hallway, arms folded. "Media is still questioning your knee."

"It's their job to ask questions. We both know that."

"You're a half step slow on defense. When was the last time you had it looked at?"

"Recently. Why? You think you can take me?"

He sighs. "My job is to understand everything about this team so we have the pieces in place to win. None of us can predict the future, but I do expect your cooperation and transparency."

"Transparency?" I echo.

I learned early I have to look out for my own problems because no one will do it for me.

His face tightens, and I know he's thinking of the same thing I am.

"What happened back in college was for the best," he says, but there's an edge of uncertainty.

"For you, maybe. I'm gonna have the back of every guy in a Kodiak jersey because they deserve it, and I'm not a guy who holds back his teammates. But you'll understand why transparency isn't something I owe you in this lifetime." I turn and head back to the court.

Chloe's still there, and I can't resist lashing out. "Wouldn't you rather sit in Jay's lap?"

She flips me off. "Mari's sister is on her way over. At least pretend you're capable of not being an asshole for a moment for Nova's sake."

I straighten.

After the other night at Red Rocks, I was amped.

Especially when Nova looked up at me in the car like all she wanted was for me to touch her.

When she kissed me, I tried to resist, but she caught me with my guard down.

If Nova had stripped in the car, or offered to blow me, or any number of other moves, I would've been able to push her away.

Instead, she brushed her sweet mouth over mine, and I found myself wanting her more than anything.

So, I kissed her back. She felt so damned good, her body soft and inviting against mine. I wanted to slide my hands under her clothes and find out what other secrets she's hiding. Wanted to kiss her until she wore me like an invisible brand.

But my only priority is basketball. It can't happen again. That's why I pulled back when all I wanted was to keep going.

Then why did I offer to help?

Because she's had a hard time. I don't like seeing people kicked when they're down.

I can have her back and spend time around her without degenerating into a caveman. I'll prove it today.

After practice wraps and Coach dismisses us, I look up to see Nova standing next to Chloe on the sidelines.

She's wearing a denim jacket over a black T-shirt, plus leggings that hug every curve. Her pink hair falls straight to her shoulders. When our eyes meet, I can tell she's been watching me a minute.

The world gets brighter.

"Hey," she says, sounding out of breath. Her lips are full and parted, and now I'm thinking of how sweet she tasted the other night.

I cross to her, stopping close enough that she has to tilt her head to hold my eyes.

I'm still angry, but the sight of her softens my edges.

"You run here?" I ask.

A delicate snort. "No."

"Whatever you say, Kodashian."

Her mouth falls open. "I'm not your groupie."

"It kind of looks like you are."

"Hey, Nova!"

Miles bounds over, parking himself next to her.

She smiles at him. "Hey, Miles."

"What are you doing here?"

"I wanted to ask Clay a few questions about the Kodiaks charity."

"Dude doesn't know shit about charity. I, on the other hand, donate plenty."

"Miles," I say, an edge in my voice.

"Wow. Sounds like I get two basketballers for the price of one." She looks between us with delight. "Why don't I come see you after I'm done with Clay?"

My hand tightens into a fist at my side.

"Yeah, all right. Lemme know when you're sick of this guy." He grins and bounds off toward Jay and Chloe.

I lean close to her ear. "You won't need anyone else when I'm done with you."

She stares up at me. "That a fact?"

"I'm twice the man he is."

Her expression is innocent and smug at once. "We'll see."

My dick twitches in my shorts.

I was bracing myself for the sweet, vulnerable Nova of the other night.

Teasing, sassy Nova is a whole new problem.

I nod to Miles without breaking eye contact with her. "Get us a ball."

He does, and I motion her over to the court.

"I'm not athletic," she warns.

"'Athletic' is inclusive by definition. I got kids at that camp who use a wheelchair, and they're plenty athletic."

Her eyes light up. "What else can you tell me about the charity?"

I watch her slide an elastic off her wrist and carefully pull back her hair.

My gaze lingers there a moment as I imagine holding her hair back with my hands.

"I play with the kids," I say. "I went this summer during off-season. It's a great facility, fresh air. You'd like it."

"Maybe I'll have to visit." She looks around the court. "This what you do—teach people to play?"

"You're the only one over age twelve."

"So, I'm special." She preens.

"Apparently."

If she had the first idea how much she affects me, it'd be game over. For both of us.

I start to dribble the ball, but she's watching me.

"It doesn't say that in your profile. Maybe people would cut you more slack about being difficult if they knew."

"Maybe I don't give a shit if people cut me slack or not."

I pass to her and motion for her to dribble like I did.

Her brows pull together as though she's not letting me get away with that answer. But finally, she relents and starts to move with the basketball.

"Like this?"

"Yeah. Now look up. At me, not the ball."

Nova does and immediately dribbles onto her foot.

"Oh crap."

I retrieve the ball easily with one outstretched hand and pass it back.

"You kids need more players. That isn't a three-on-three," Jayden calls from the side.

Brooke's in one of the seats, legs crossed and flashing red-soled heels. "I'm not dressed for this."

"Right, excuses to avoid getting your ass kicked," Jay replies. "Girls can't beat boys."

"That's it. You're going down." She lunges toward her brother, trying to get him in a headlock and failing.

Chloe's already stepping out of her shoes and shrugging her jacket onto a chair.

Miles hollers, "Hell yeah."

I grin.

Two minutes later, the six of us are playing.

Jay, Miles, and I are still sweaty from practice, our jerseys stuck to our bodies.

Chloe brings it up the court, her shoes discarded out of bounds. Jay's watching her, but she's watching all of us at once. He says something to distract her, and she shakes him off.

Miles is on Brooke. She feints one way, then cuts to get a pass from Chloe.

"Suckers," Brooke crows.

"Crossovers in a skirt!" Chloe calls.

Brooke grins as she takes Miles deep into the paint.

He's got his hands full.

"They're good," Nova murmurs.

I'm inches away. Because I'm guarding her, I have an excuse to get even closer. "Chloe was MVP and state champion in high school. Brooke's played since she was six because her brother made her. She's still one of the only people who can guard him because she knows what he's thinking before he does."

"Everyone in the league gives him too much credit. He doesn't think at all," Brooke tosses.

"That's cold, sis," Jay calls from where he's on Chloe.

Brooke squares up toward Nova, nodding. I let Nova get the ball. She dribbles around me. When she turns to shoot it, she's not set up. No way it's going in.

I reach around her and grab the ball with one hand. I could take it without touching her, but I wrap the other arm around her shoulders and drag her back against my body.

"FOUL!!" Chloe and Brooke holler.

"No way," Miles protests while Jay's cracking up.

Now I've got the ball, and Nova's pulled tight against me.

"What happens now?" she murmurs, her voice full of anticipation. Her body vibrates against mine, and all I want to do is hold her there.

But I can't, because it's wrong, and I promised I wouldn't. Not to mention how hard I'd get roasted by everyone present.

So, I pull her to the line opposite the basket.

"This is the free throw line."

"You get it in from here?" she wonders.

I smirk and set her up one step at a time. She takes a deep breath and lobs the ball, missing by a mile.

With a couple of steps, I intercept the ball and grab it out of the air before it can hit the ground. It's in her hands the next second. "This time, use your legs."

"She's five-five!" Chloe contends, shoving Jay's shoulder. "Let her shoot from closer."

"She doesn't need to," I toss back, confident in her ability. "Do you, Pink?"

She sets her teeth, shakes her head.

"That's it. Bend your knees. Power comes from your lower body. Trust me." I step behind her again and run my hand down her side, skimming over her curved ass to her thighs as a reminder of what she can do. "Lower, like this."

The next throw swooshes through the hoop like it's powered by invisible angels.

"Yes!" Nova exclaims, pumping her fists in the air.

I barely have time to process my satisfaction before she throws her arms around me in a celebratory hug.

I should resist.

Instead, I wrap my arms around her and return the hug, every soft curve of her body lining up against mine.

It feels good, holding her. Better than anything I've felt in a long time.

We're not skin to skin but her heart hammers against mine, her warmth making me wonder how much is from the exercise and how much is from our proximity.

When I set her back down on steady feet, our faces are close—as close as they can be considering I'm a foot taller anyway.

"That was incredible," she murmurs, her bright eyes so stunningly blue I could drown in them.

She's not for me.

But with each smile, I believe it less.

I take a moment to soak her in and revel in our victory before turning away.

See? I can keep it together. Don't need to grope her or kiss her or imagine what it would be like to hear her whisper, "That was incredible," when I'm done fucking her senseless.

"Nova, you're almost as good at basketball as you are at drawing," Brooke comments.

The flush that crawls up her cheeks is from more than exertion.

My curiosity is piqued. "Drawing? What do you draw?"

"All kinds of things."

Interesting.

"I'll take a shot from anywhere in this half of the court. With my eyes closed. I make this shot, you show me everything," I say.

Her face screws up. "From anywhere?"

I nod.

She positions me just shy of half court.

I size up the basket, then square my feet.

Everyone's watching.

I shut my eyes and take a breath before sending the ball up.

I don't need the hollers that erupt to know it went in.

12

NOVA

When I get back from the stadium, I park in the massive driveway before heading inside.

I told Clay I didn't have my sketchbook on me and I'd show him another time.

The way he dragged my body against his, surrounding me with his heat, his length. Every nerve in my body was throbbing.

Not to mention how he made that basket with his eyes closed.

For an instant, I wasn't the girl who doesn't matter lusting after the hot superstar.

I enjoy being around him, but only if I can stay on even ground. I won't let myself be drawn in, be weak and gullible.

But the second Clay sees the drawing of him, he'll know how fascinated I am by him.

It's nearly dinnertime, and my stomach growls. The lights are on in the kitchen, and I head in there. The chef is probably nearly done.

But it's Mari who lifts her head from the oven.

We've barely spoken two words since the day of the dress fitting. She's been busy with work before taking time off for the wedding, but it's still been cold.

Spending time at the court gave me the courage to try and put things right.

"Smells good in here," I venture, leaning against the granite island. "Did the chef go on strike?"

Mari sets the oven mitts on the counter and turns to face me. She swipes a piece of hair from her face.

"When Harlan and I started dating, we'd both come home after a long day and cook together with a bottle of wine." She smiles. "He wasn't a GM then. He was still trying for his big break."

"I didn't realize."

"This is his first NBA GM job. He needs to do well."

"I couldn't find the merlot" —Harlan's voice comes from the other doorway that heads downstairs—"but I've got a cab that will make you—"

Mari clears her throat.

"Oh. Hi, Nova." He looks between us, sizing up the situation. "Let me give you ladies a moment."

He opens the wine and pours two glasses,

handing them to us before grabbing a third for himself.

"I didn't know you cooked," I comment.

"Not much since taking over the team. I spend most of my day getting grown men to agree on how to win basketball games."

I think about the tension between him and Clay that he alluded to the day I arrived. It's probably a misunderstanding, just a matter of people who want the same thing going about it in different ways.

"Do they get to see you like this? At home, relaxed?" I prompt. "I bet they'd love to be included."

He looks at Mari and something passes between them.

"That's an excellent idea." Harlan takes his glass out the door to the living room.

"He's pretty great," I murmur.

"The best. I knew he was the one the first time I tried to cook for him and he said only if he could help."

She turns toward the stove, and I round the island to peek at what's in the oven.

"Lasagna. Yum."

"It's vegan with zucchini noodles. Dairy messes me up. I'd be out of commission all night from the cheese."

"Since when?"

"Since I moved to Colorado."

I turn that over.

"About the other day. I didn't mean to spring that on you," I say.

"I don't understand what went down. You lost your job. And Brad."

"He left the firm. And me," I add.

"How are you not freaking out about this?"

"Brad or work?"

"Both. I can't believe you're here, trying cakes and dresses when you don't even know if you have a job to go back to."

"They're reviewing the circumstances. They'll realize I wasn't involved and give me my job back. It just takes time."

They have to give me my job back, I remind myself.

She picks up her glass and takes a long drink. "Were you and Brad even engaged?"

"We were." I grab my wine, too, squeezing the stem too hard. The feel of the ring on my finger is almost gone but not quite. "He asked me the month before. I wanted to tell you, but I figured I'd see you this fall and wanted to surprise you in person."

"But?"

"But he stole money. They assumed because of our relationship that I might be in on it. That's why they put me on leave pending an investigation.

"Brad had been wanting my help updating some client files, including billings. He had some big clients who retained him for multiple properties, and he was always making deals to save them money. Or so I thought. One day, one of them came asking questions. The next week, he was gone."

Her eyes round in horror. "What about at home? There was no warning?"

Smiles that went as easily as they came.

Careless attention except when he was in his office.

Praise only when I did what he wanted.

I take a sip of my wine, the warm red flowing smoothly across my tongue.

"Maybe I should have known." When I see how affectionate Harlan is with Mari, it reminds me how different Brad and I were.

"After we moved in together, I was so happy to be with him that I never questioned how things were. That when he took me to an industry event on his arm, it felt like a favor. He was successful and normal, and I wanted him to want me. I spent so much time trying that I never stopped to ask what it meant that he didn't already want me."

Mari crosses to the fridge and pulls out a bag of prewashed lettuce and a pepper. "I'm sorry."

I grab a cutting board and a knife and set both on the counter, then hold up both hands. "It's fine."

She tosses me the pepper, then gets a bowl for the lettuce.

It's not fine exactly, but I don't know how to have

that conversation with my sister. We haven't talked that openly in a long time.

Plus, for the first time today, I forgot about what happened. For hours.

Playing basketball was so much fun. I felt as though I was part of something. The way Clay included me, and taught me, and touched me...

Mari looks up. "I guess I take for granted that Mom and Dad cared about each other. Nothing else was stable, but I never questioned that."

I start to chop the pepper in rhythmic slices.

"Remember when Dad learned to play the ukulele so he had an instrument while Mom sang?" she asks.

Nostalgia rocks me. "Yes. Mom had the most beautiful voice."

"She used to sing that song. 'Home.' Whenever I had a bad day, she'd sing it to me."

"I better than remember it. I recorded it."

Her eyes round with nostalgia. "Really? Do you have it?"

"I'll find it." I make a mental note.

"We could use it in the wedding," she goes on. "As part of the ceremony."

"That's a great idea!"

Mari sighs happily. "I want you to find a good man. Someone who can take care of you."

My smile fades. "Did it ever occur to you that I can take care of myself?"

"No. From the time we were kids, you'd chase butterflies and sing songs and draw pictures. You got to be careless and irresponsible. It was my job to keep you safe, to protect you."

It takes a moment for that to sink in. I always knew she was more together than me but hadn't realized how much that bothered her.

"Not anymore," I vow. "I know you were passed over for that promotion when you came to help me out last year. You can stop saving me. I want to be here for you. But you have to give me a chance. Okay?"

My sister studies me for a moment. "Okay."

13

NOVA

The first preseason game is full of energy and promise. Signs and pennants draped around the stadium proclaim "KODIAK NATION!" in huge caps. The stadium is packed with fans, plenty of whom are wearing purple-and-gold team jerseys or shirts with the words "BEAR FORCE" printed across them.

"What's Bear Force?" I call to Brooke as we make our way into a box in one corner of the stadium.

"That's what the team's superfans call themselves."

"It looks sold out."

"Yup. The entire city wants to see if your boy's gonna give us a comeback year."

"He's not mine," I say as we take our seats.

"Right, you go around drawing random guys like you want to bang them." She shoots me a look.

Well, I guess that answers whether she knew the sketch was Clay.

"Has he seen your outfit?" Brooke gestures to my jersey.

I glance down at the one Miles gave me. "What? It says 'Kodiaks.'"

She laughs silently, but I don't get the joke.

Since I played with her and the guys, I've been busy helping with the wedding. One of the hotels hosting visitors double-booked, so I called around to find a bed and breakfast for some out-of-town guests. We also finalized the invitation list for the bachelorette, which we're hoping to hold at the Four Seasons Spa. The florist called and said it wasn't looking good for importing the exotic roses Mari insisted she wanted, but we can figure that out tomorrow.

"It was fun to play basketball with you guys. Nice of Clay to be patient with me."

Brooke sweeps her hair over her shoulder, brows arching. "I've known Clay for years. He's a lot of things. Grouchy. Unyielding. Un-fucking-believable on the court. Nice isn't one of them."

A little thrill chases up my spine.

So yeah, when I think about Clay, I get hot.

Maybe more than hot.

He's got issues of his own, but hearing him talk about his work with the charity made me realize there's more to him than the media makes out.

In the past couple of days, we've been texting here and there. He says he's keeping me out of trouble. I say I'm trying to make sure he gets his laugh a day whether he wants it or not.

But I'm excited to see him in person, even if it's from a distance. I can't wait to watch him tear up the court, and when Brooke asked if I was planning to go, it was an easy yes.

We're here a few minutes before tip-off. Apparently, Harlan watches all the games from downstairs, but Mari and Chloe said they'd meet us later for drinks.

The place is already buzzing, and Brooke's words dial up my excitement another notch.

I texted an hour ago to wish Clay luck but didn't hear back. He's probably in some pregame routine.

Now, the lights go dark, and the crowd erupts before they come up again. Players are announced one at a time, the opposing team's so unceremoniously it seems unfair and the Kodiaks' with the utmost enthusiasm.

Rookie.

Atlas.

Miles.

Jayden.

Clay.

When he's introduced, the building shakes.

I've seen him in his jersey in press images and online, but this feels different.

When I scan the crowd, there are hundreds of people wearing his jersey. Possibly thousands.

Wow.

I knew he was a star. But here, he's a god.

"You watch any basketball before?" Brooke asks.

I shake my head. "No."

The basketball goes up in the middle of the court, and both teams swat at it.

From then on, she explains what I'm seeing.

It's five-on-five. Each player has a position, frontcourt or backcourt, but they help each other out as needed over the forty-eight minutes.

"Some of the guys are fast and nimble, able to cut and shoot from distance, like Jay," Brooke goes on. "Others are huge, tall enough to grab a ball off the rim, wide enough to block offensive players, like Atlas.

"Then there's Clay, who's got both—height and strength, plus the moves to score from anywhere he wants."

But when she starts talking about schemes and coverages, I shake my head.

"You're not remembering this, are you?" she asks dryly.

"You had me up to fouls," I say truthfully.

"There are three more preseason games. We'll go over the rest next time."

Next time.

Thinking that there will be another game,

another chance to experience this atmosphere, makes my heart swell with joy.

I settle back into watching the team, who has a few miscommunications but eventually manages to pull off a dazzling passing play that has Jayden finding Clay for an emphatic dunk—the crowd around us erupts in celebration.

I'm on my feet, too, screaming.

By the end of the first half, the Kodiaks are ahead by ten.

When the clock runs out, they win by eighteen.

The arena is deafening, and my chest feels like it's going to burst from the thrill of it.

"What happens now?" I ask, still feeling the adrenaline rush that comes with a win as the arena starts to drain of its delirious fans.

"Coach and a couple players will have media." Brooke's eyes sparkle with excitement. "We can pop in and say congratulations."

She leads me back down through the narrow corridors, the walls pulsing with the energy of the crowd still lingering, and past security, who lets her around a corner and into a doorless room with a knowing nod.

"Wait, are we in the..." I trail off before saying, "Dressing room."

Brooke holds her hand over her eyes like a shield to protect herself from what she might see inside. "Is my brother naked in here?"

"I'm supposed to assess that?" But I look around and see a few faces I don't recognize amongst the sweaty sports gear that fills the air with its musky scent. "Nope, you're safe."

Brooke drops her hand as Miles rolls up wearing only a white towel that hugs tightly against his toned body, his hair damp and slicked back.

"The women's changing room is... Scratch that, we don't have one. Nice jersey, Nova."

"Thanks. You guys played great," I say, my voice full of admiration.

"Appreciate that." His smile is wide and genuine.

Brooke rolls her eyes. "My brother around? Or Clay?"

"Still at media." Miles is handsome in a roguishly charming way, like you'd have no hope of checking him out without being caught.

But as much as he's objectively hot, a spark of arousal doesn't rise within me like it does when I'm around Clay.

"You seen Waffles?" Miles asks, and Brooke and I shake our heads in unison. "His new dog sitter is supposed to be around. He's been going through 'em like crazy."

We head out and turn the corner to find Jayden and Clay in the hall. Brooke throws her arms around her brother in delight. "You survived!"

"Hope I did you proud." He smiles warmly at his sister before turning to me.

I focus on Clay, who looks breathtakingly sexy in a dark hoodie, his damp hair curling around his ears. Like he just stepped out of the shower after slaying a dragon. I suppose to the fans, it's true.

His gaze is so intense that I have to force myself to hold it.

"Hi," I say.

"You came." His attention flicks briefly to my jersey, then back to my face.

"Yeah. Congrats on the win."

"Thanks."

But Clay's expression is unreadable now, shuttered and guarded as if I'm some stranger he just met instead of the woman he kissed in his car and has been texting ever since.

"I'll see you around."

Heart pounding in my chest, I watch him walk down the hall past Brooke and Jayden, who're still talking animatedly.

I'm left feeling crushed and rejected, like he stomped on me with his massive shoe for no reason at all.

∼

Dear Kodiaks players, executives, and staff:

You are cordially invited to a barbeque at the home of Harlan and Mari.

4:30PM Sunday

Please RSVP

∼

14

NOVA

Harlan wasted zero time "implementing my idea," to quote him, of letting the players behind the curtain. Apparently, the way to do that is host a spur-of-the-moment backyard event involving the entire organization.

But when Mari got her hands on it, she insisted that adding a few VIPs from the Denver business community was the best use of their sprawling scenery.

While I was pleased Harlan took my suggestion, my first thought was whether one player in particular would be gracing us with his growly, sexy presence.

Thursday's game was nothing short of a disaster. Clay acted as if I was some stranger he had never met before, treating me with a distant, icy coolness. And I was sure that he had seen my red face and burning cheeks, too embarrassed to do anything but stand there like an idiot.

He's texted me a handful of times since. I didn't feel like answering. Getting my heart stomped on twice in one week is not my idea of a good time.

I'm questioning whether Clay will even show up today. Probably not for Harlan's sake, and he doesn't strike me as the garden-party type. The knowledge should be a comfort, but it only makes me feel worse.

The caterers arrived around eight in the morning and began unloading their supplies while I helped Mari get everything ready.

At almost noon, I'm about to go change into some cut-off shorts when Mari says, "Hey, tell me you're not wearing that?"

My heart drops as I glance down at my outfit – a ruffled tank and jeans. "What's wrong with this?"

Mari rolls her eyes. "You look like a caterer. The *mayor* is coming, Nova."

Nowhere did it say "fancy outfit" on the list of items to prepare. Then again, Mari did invite the entire Denver business community.

I go upstairs and strip down to my bra and thong to sort through my clothes, dismissing one item after another. I'm not sure I brought anything appropriate for this event. Hell, even the limited contents of my tiny apartment closet in Boston might not have fit the bill.

Suddenly, a sharp knock comes on my door, and

it swings open before I can even attempt to cover myself. Brooke stands in the doorway, looking stylish and polished in a high-necked coral minidress.

"Is that what you're wearing? Bold choice," she says as I cover my exposed chest. "But, if you've got it, flaunt it."

I laugh. "I'm not sure I have it."

"Are you kidding?" Her gaze scans my body. "You're gorgeous."

My hands fall to my sides. If it's not weird for her, I guess it's not for me either. I don't have any particular hang-ups about my figure, but I've never had the all-out confidence some women have.

"I'm surprised you're not in stilettos," I say.

Brooke crosses to my bed and sits gracefully on it.

"Wedges are lawn friendly. As much as I like to skewer people, I leave the ground intact." Her legs cross, and she folds her hands on top of them, beaming. "If you don't have something to wear, I brought options. I'm getting photographed, and I need to look good against the backdrop."

"That sounds amazing."

"Done."

She rises and leaves the room.

I'm not sure why she's so keen to help me, but I'm grateful for the save.

Three short minutes later, she returns with a long garment bag slung over her arm, which she drops unceremoniously onto my bed. She unzips it with a flourish and pulls out a cream-colored floral dress with a deep neckline and tiny capped sleeves.

My eyes widen in shock at the gorgeous garment. "That's beautiful."

"Put it on."

Gingerly taking it from her outstretched hands, I slip on the dress and pair it with a set of nude wedges. When I turn to look at myself in the mirror, whatever words I had evaporate.

"Wow," is all I say as Brooke zips me up completely.

"Accurate."

The dress clings to my curves, hugging my breasts and nipping in at my waist before ending in a flirty hemline that teases my thighs. I preen in the mirror, pleased with the way I look. With wild pink hair and soft eye makeup, I feel like a garden fairy.

"What if I want to sit down?" I ask Brooke with a hint of apprehension.

"This is not a sitting down dress," she says with a laugh as she adjusts my hair.

"I'm not trying to impress anyone," I explain. "I just don't want to be mistaken for a waiter."

"So, there's no grumpy all-star you want checking you out?" Brooke teases.

Cautiously, I peek out the window, watching as groups of people start gathering on the lawn below.

"He's probably not coming."

But then I spot him, standing with a couple of the guys from the team and looking unfairly handsome, and my traitorous heart skips a beat.

"It kind of looks like he did," Brooke whispers.

15

CLAY

"This is nice," Rookie says, looking around Harlan's massive backyard. "Free shrimp. Though I figured there'd be more girls here."

The barbeque is a power move. A blatant excuse to show off while also sucking up.

There's only one girl I'm thinking about, and she hasn't answered my texts.

"Clay, right?" Harlan's fiancée, Mari, steps into the group and smiles at me. She's wearing a sleek dress and heels and looks nothing like Nova. "The mayor is here. I'd love to introduce you."

"We've met." I look past her at the suits who're rubbing elbows and glad-handing one another.

I hate the politics. Better left to Harlan and ownership. If I wanted to be involved in that shit, I would've majored in kissing ass in college.

She tries again. "Then surely you'll want to catch

up. Come on. These people make it possible for the team to play in Denver. The red tape they cut, the money they invest—"

"You know how much comes into this team through media rights? We bring money to the city, not the other way around. Thanks for the invite, but I'm gonna pass."

Mari's eyes narrow, and I turn away and head back to some of the guys.

"Careful. You won't be invited back," Jay comments.

"That a promise?"

If I'm extra pissy today, it's because she's not the sister I want to see.

Nova's been dodging me the last three days.

Well, she can't avoid me forever.

Jay's attention is captured by something behind me.

I turn, expecting to see Chloe.

It's not Chloe.

Nova's on the other side of the lawn talking with Brooke.

Her hair falls in waves that brush her collarbone, which is exposed by the dress a few shades darker than her skin and ends mid-thigh.

"Wow, she looks hot," Jay drawls. "You know she'd be here?"

She laughs on the other side of the lawn, and my abs clench.

"I figured, but we haven't talked in a few days."

"Since you were a prick at the game."

I frown. "I wasn't."

"You were," Jay says.

I saw her for a second after our first game, but I was in a bad mood.

My knee was giving me shit.

Then seeing her in another guy's jersey, even my teammate's, pissed me off more.

She's not mine. Not my girl, not my problem.

"Good thing Clayton Wade doesn't have time for dating." Jay claps a hand on my shoulder. "Because it looks like you missed your chance."

When I search Nova out with my eyes once more, Brooke's gone. In her place is...

Miles.

I shove my drink at Jay's chest. "Hold this."

I cut through the crowd.

"Hey, Clay," Miles says.

"Jay needs to talk to you."

"Really?" Nova leans in. "Because Jayden looks just fine to me."

I glance back to see him laughing with Atlas. *Fuck.* "Miles. Get out of here, or this piece of advice is the last assist I'm giving you for the entire season."

He blinks, then heads toward the bar.

When I turn back, Nova's arms are folded over her chest. "You can't keep cutting in."

"On your epic romance with Miles?"

Her lips twitch in profile. "I told you, we're—"

"If you say 'destined,' I'm going to punch a hole in his face."

"Sounds like you could use therapy."

"I'm in therapy."

She looks over in surprise.

A waiter hands me champagne, and I take two and pass her one.

The ring of a knife striking a glass calls everyone's attention to the front. Harlan drones on about how good it is to have everyone here, especially with the season starting soon.

I step closer to Nova. "You owe me a drawing."

"I don't owe you anything. You barely said two words to me the other day."

"I was in game mode."

"You were in asshole mode."

I blink at her. I'm not used to people calling me out.

"That's just how it goes during the season. Things get intense. It was nothing personal."

She scans the crowd behind me. "When you saw me," she murmurs, "it was like a switch flipped and you shut down. You didn't want to see me. So, it's probably easier if you don't."

Harlan finishes his speech, and the crowd applauds.

"Easier for who?" I demand under my breath.

She doesn't answer.

Nova thinks it's better if we don't hang out.

That's bullshit.

It's like asking me to unsee her. To forget how it feels to be near her. Even now, standing a few inches away with her freezing me out, is better than that.

I'm deciding how to convince her without starting a scene when I pick up a conversation between guests a few feet behind us.

"... his fiancée is lovely and accomplished. Mari's parents died suddenly a few years back, but she's carried a huge load since. It sounds like her sister's a total deadweight."

Nova heard it, too.

Her face goes white, lips pressed together. She spins on her heel and heads for the house.

I curse, glaring at the unsuspecting guests.

She might not want anything to do with me anymore, but I'm not done with her.

I follow her through the doors at the back of the house.

People are milling about, and I scan the interior before I see a pair of curvy legs ascending one set of the double staircases.

I opt for the other, taking the stairs two at a time.

At the top, I start down the long hall.

I find the room with the closed door. "Nova."

There's no answer.

"Come on, I know you're in there."

Still nothing.

I reach for the handle and push the door wide to find a bedroom. She's nowhere in sight, but there's a sketchpad on the desk. I flip it open.

On top is a drawing of me playing basketball.

Then another.

Another.

It's a punch in the gut. Not only that she's been drawing me with a wild intensity bordering on obsession, but that they're drawn so intimately. In these drawings, there's none of the hopelessness I feel.

I look up, scanning the room until my attention lands on a closed door.

A closet or bathroom.

"These drawings are really good," I call through the door.

Maybe I can get her talking, to lower her defenses and tell me what the hell is going on.

There's no answer.

I'm not used to getting the run around.

"Sure, I'm a little surprised I'm wearing clothes in these, but there must be another sketchpad somewhere…"

I hear the click of Nova unlocking the door.

Her face is at the crack, flushed.

She leans her temple against the door. "I'm not Mari. I'm not organized and put together. But I'm not a mess."

"I know you're not."

Her eyes are tinged with red, and I want to hit whoever made her cry.

"For a long time after my parents died, I couldn't draw. Starting up again was hard."

"How'd it feel when you did?"

"Like home." She blinks up at me, her lashes dark and damp.

I step closer, nudge the door open another inch. "Basketball used to feel like home for me. It doesn't anymore."

Her fingers tighten on the wood. "How does it feel?"

This, right here, is dangerous. I'm crossing a threshold I didn't realize I was at. If I give words to the dark emotions colliding in my chest, I'll unleash something I can't put back.

"Like I'm drowning," I say. "Like I'm seconds from sinking to the bottom of the ocean and all I can do is postpone the inevitable."

Her blue eyes bore into mine so deeply I swear she can see everything I'm feeling.

She pulls back the door.

I should be outside with my teammates. Or rehabbing my body. Or working with my agent to make this trade happen.

Instead, I step into the bathroom.

It's white and wood and cozy. I take in her toothbrush and makeup bag leaning on the vanity against the mirror. Little feminine details. We have so little in common, but she's the one I'm seeking out.

"During the game, I came down after a dunk and my knee screamed. I didn't say anything to the trainers. Didn't let it show. But I was up in my head over it."

"That must be scary. But players get hurt all the time. Isn't it a risk you take?"

"Yeah, but most of them aren't as good as me. There's not as much riding on it." I hang my head. "Back in college, I was in it with this girl and found out she was cheating on me. I spiralled, it got bad, and it almost ended my basketball career." Her eyes deepen with empathy, but she lets me continue. "I was in a dark place. I pulled out of it, but I could have just as easily not. Everything I worked for my entire life would've been wasted."

I swallow, tasting bitterness in my throat. I've never told anyone all of that except Jay, and even he doesn't know the details.

Her lips curve softly. "We all have soft spots, Clay. In our bodies, our hearts, our souls. That's how we know we're human."

Nova doesn't judge me, or pity me, or tell me I'm selfish. Her words release some of the heaviness in my chest.

"I know you think I'm stupid for wanting to be here for Mari," she goes on. "But my sister is the only person I have left who cares about me."

She crosses to the window, gazing out like an angel watching humans below. Guests flood the lawn, little specks of color bright against the green grass.

"That's not true," I say, coming up behind her.

Nova's head turns as she glances toward me. Her hair brushes my shirt as she flexes her wrist absently.

I shouldn't want sweet and innocent. She's the last person I need in my way.

But right now, so help me, it's all I want.

"It isn't?" she asks.

I shake my head.

Her attention drops to my mouth, and I want to put it on her everywhere she'll let me.

A feeling flickers to life in my chest that hasn't been there in a long time.

Not a spark.

It's her.

She's under my skin, in my blood.

Her breasts rise and fall with her shallow breathing. The dress looks thin enough that I could feel her warmth through it. I want to close the last inch between us and find out.

I reach for her wrist. My thumb probes her skin, the veins beneath.

Nova lets out a little hiss.

"Still hurt?" I ask.

"No."

She's soft, her skin pale.

I bend to brush my lips over her wrist. "How about now?"

She sucks in a breath.

Desire flares to life, the flickering flame of attraction becoming a roaring inferno. It's not the kind I'm used to, a shallow heat that fades as fast as it burns.

I give a shit about her.

Give so many shits it's a wonder I have any shits left.

"After the game," she starts, "you were a prick."

"You're right," I admit.

"Next time, say, 'Nova, my knee hurts like hell, and I'm in a terrible mood.'"

"I didn't like seeing you in his jersey."

She cocks her head, surprised. "What was I supposed to wear?"

I take her chin in my fingers, lifting it so she's forced to look me dead in the eyes.

"Wear mine," I murmur. "Next time you wear a jersey to a game, you fucking wear mine."

Her eyes widen.

I can't give her what she deserves because my career comes first, but for a second, I imagine being the man who could.

We stand there staring at each other until music rings out in the yard below.

"Nova!" A woman's voice calls from somewhere in the house.

Nova jumps. "We should get back out there."

I want to lock the door and lose myself in this girl.

I want to let myself imagine there's a world where someone sees me as I am, as I could be, and neither of those have anything to do with my busted knee or how many points I score.

I step back to let her past, and she starts toward the door. "Clay?"

The way she says my name makes me want to drag her back and slam the door behind us.

"Yeah?"

Her lips curve. "Thank you."

I'm so fucked.

16

NOVA

"That was some barbeque." Mari sighs as she sinks into an overstuffed chair in front of the fireplace later that night. "Do you think the mayor had a good time?"

"How could he not?" Harlan offers with a smile.

"I wanted Clay to charm some of them," she says, and my attention perks up. "He wasn't very accommodating. Maybe he's incapable of charm."

"Or maybe it's not his job."

Two sets of eyes land on me.

I say, "You don't need to pimp him out. Or any of them."

"Harlan has all kinds of pressures on him running this team. It's the least they can do."

"Yeah, but Harlan doesn't actually have to play basketball and have a camera in his face every second of the workday. No offense."

Mari frowns at me. "What the hell has got into you?"

"Nothing." I flash a smile and head toward the backyard, where staff are still cleaning up from the event.

After today, I have energy to burn.

I started out feeling intimidated and out of place, but now I'm energized.

I glance up at the window I was pressed against earlier.

Heat floods me, desire that makes my breasts tingle and heat pool between my thighs at the memory of being so close to him.

I want him and he wants me. That much is obvious, even if it still blows my mind.

For a moment, I thought he was going to slam me against the wall and take me like in one of my morning fantasies.

This feeling inside me has less to do with me and everything to do with Clay. His confidence is contagious. The way he doesn't give a shit what anyone else thinks.

I go upstairs and take a shower. My wrist still hums from his lips.

It felt as if a knot came loose in my chest.

I think of what he told me about his struggles in college. It explains a lot about why he's so self-contained and why he doesn't trust easily.

His compliment on my art was amazing. When

he said that it was good, I wanted to dismiss it, but a deeper part of me wanted to say:

I know.

I know I'm capable.

I know I can do this.

As much as I could turn into a puddle and spend the entire night replaying my time with Clay in my mind, I have things to do. After stepping out of the shower, I fold my hair in a towel and look at my sketchpad, still open to the images of him.

I grab my phone on the dresser to switch on some music, then spot a text.

Brooke: Did the dress get you the princess moment you wanted?

I bite my lip.

Nova: I'll have it cleaned and back to you soon.

Brooke: If you got it that dirty, I'll take that as a yes ;)

Nova: Thank you.

Brooke: That's what friends are for.

I laugh. I could be friends with Brooke. She's smart and fun, plus she's kind and looks for the best in everyone.

I cross to my window seat, pull out my phone, and bring up the charity information Harlan sent.

The proposal is to add a program to help prepare teens from disadvantaged backgrounds for adult life, including finding jobs.

I have no doubt it would hit close to home for Mari, but I wonder how much they talk about the reason for that.

Next, I navigate to the Kodiaks' camp website.

The camp looks fabulous. The more I look, the more interested I am, and not only for Mari. It's amazing the team invests so much. I get that it's a PR activity, but the kids are clearly having an incredible time. They're laughing and fitting in and trying new things.

Maybe Clay's right and I've spent too much time sitting on the sidelines. I need to act.

No more putting my future in others' hands. No more silently waiting on the design firm to investigate what happened with Brad.

I'm going to request an update on my leave and remind them I had nothing to do with the fraud.

I pull open a new email message and address it to the head of HR.

A few minutes later, I take a deep breath and hit Send.

17

CLAY

"We've got movement." My agent's voice comes over the crackling phone.

"Tell me." The sun bakes my neck as I pace from my car to the office building. It's a fair distance from my condo, but I have a solid reason for making the drive.

"There's interest from Phoenix. And Boston."

"That's it?" I yank open the door and stalk to the stairwell. I don't want to be seen in the elevator, though staff are discreet. Normally, I'll tolerate requests for selfies and autographs, but not today.

"Last week, I would've said yes. But I just got a call from LA."

My grip tightens. "And?"

"They're interested. They caught the game, plus some workout tape."

I take the stairs two at a time. Even the four flights won't have me breaking a sweat. The benefits of fitness and all. "How'd they get that?"

"I sent it to them."

At the top, I step into the main hallway and stop in front of a hardwood door with a brass plaque on the front.

"They make Harlan an offer?" I ask.

"Not yet. I think they want to see how the preseason shakes down and how your knee holds up."

I grimace. *Wait and see.* It's management's favorite setting. As if basketball is some comprehensible system and all the unknowns will become clear with just a little more time.

"Maybe they're concerned you're not back to a hundred percent. That the injury's going to flare up."

"They're wrong."

"Course they are. They want to watch a few games, that's all."

I click off.

The twinge of discomfort I felt in our first game was back in practice today. Not that I told anyone. I played through it, and I'll keep playing through it.

A text appears on my phone from Nova with one word:

Done.

I click it and find the drawing she started. It sucks the air from my chest. She finished the one of me on the bench. There's skill in every stroke, but there's knowing, too.

Nova's been living rent free in my head ever since the barbeque.

The way she opened up for me, the way she hummed when my lips stroked her skin, it only made me want more.

"Clay."

I look up to see my therapist hovering in the doorway.

"You're right on time."

I follow him inside. A few minutes later, I'm taking up half of his couch, and he's perched in his chair.

"Good to see you. It's been a little while."

"Someone reminded me talking can help."

If I'm going to spend any more time around Nova, I can't shut her out like I did after the game.

And I do want to spend time around her. With all that's going on, I've decided not to look too hard at the reasons.

She's here for her sister. And me, I've got shit to figure out. My career comes first, but I can't kick the idea that there could be more to me than basketball.

"How was the game?" he asks.

"It was a win."

"But?"

I tug on the cord in my hoodie and clench my jaw, searching for the words to explain the team's stagnation. "It's not enough. This team has a ceiling, but nobody will admit it."

"Maybe they just need someone to get them going, something to focus on," he says.

I shake my head. "You either have what it takes to beat the best or you don't. We don't."

He crosses one ankle over his knee and looks at me calmly. "Maybe you think you don't have it in you to lead because you've never tried."

My heart starts to race. I can never be a leader. Being responsible for every move of an entire franchise would be too much for me to bear with a knee that still twinges with pain at the wrong movement.

I put enough expectations on myself to be the best for myself, for my career and my fans, my agent, and all the people who've gotten me where I am.

"You don't understand—I have to leave," I say, turning away from him and pacing around the room.

"Then why don't you?"

I stop pacing and face him, meeting his eye contact with a determined stare of my own. "I'm working on it."

The clock on the wall ticks loudly.

"Once you're in LA and you've won a championship, what then?"

"What do you mean?" I ask.

"You're already one of the best. Everyone agrees to it. You'd need something else to fight for."

I press the heels of my hands against my eyes. "You sound like someone else I know."

"Speaking of, how is your sister?"

"She's in grad school. Training to be like you, actually."

That'll be a treat.

"You feel guilt over what happened," he says.

"I'll always have that."

"Because you love her."

"Obviously. She's my little sister."

"But?"

"But I let her down. I was supposed to look out for her, and instead, I was doing basketball. It's the only thing I'm good at. I gave up everything for this. It's who I am. If I'm not the best, then what the fuck am I?"

"You seem more agitated than in our last few sessions. Has something changed?"

Nothing. Nothing has changed, except...

Her face flashes in my mind.

"I met a woman. It was completely random."

It felt like fate.

"She makes me question things."

Like whether basketball is the only thing I want in my life.

At the party, having Nova in my arms was the closest I've felt to freedom in a long time. I don't have to perform when I'm with her. She sees beyond the image to the man underneath.

"I want to be around her," I say.

"But?"

"But the last time I wanted to be around someone ended badly." My chest tightens as the words come out.

He shifts forward in his seat, eyes brightening. I've just fed him some prime therapist catnip shit. "What happened?"

The pain in my chest never completely goes away. It's been better over the years, but it still lingers. "I was serious about her, and she was serious about fucking the GM of our team behind my back for months."

The ache intensifies as I think of the way I felt when I found out. The hurt. The anger.

"That must have been painful."

"The organization covered it up."

In the name of winning, they hid the truth. As if I was too fragile or stupid to handle it. As if I was a machine and not a man.

It was a reminder that they valued winning more than truth or respect for me.

"And that was the start of your struggles."

I nod, my mouth dry.

What he means is it was the start of the darkest moments.

Not knowing who I wanted to be or if I even wanted to be at all. Drinking too much, sleeping all day, and avoiding workouts were just some of the ways I tried to fill the void.

My teammates began to look at me like I had no hope of recovery, and they weren't wrong.

It took Jay, who played for a rival team, to get me started on the right path again and get me back on track to Finals.

It also made me lose trust in anyone in a suit.

Ultimately, it taught me what I needed to focus on: being on the court and playing basketball with everything that I had.

"What would it take to open yourself up to connecting with another person? Without judgment or cynicism?" my therapist asks.

"A miracle."

But Nova's face appears in my mind, and despite the years of baggage and rejection of everything that's not basketball, I want to try.

18

NOVA

"Are we close?" I ask, glancing toward Clay crammed into the passenger seat.

Even with the seat pushed back as far as it can go, the car still feels too small for us both.

When I mentioned I wanted to meet with Robin, Clay offered to bring me. Tomorrow, he's flying to Atlanta for a preseason game, but until then, he's free. I said yes without hesitation, although with the condition that I could drive.

We pass rolling hills sprinkled with the odd house, and the tension builds in me.

"How much farther?" I ask.

"Turn here."

I follow his directions. "You do this all without a GPS?"

"Spent a lot of time here while I was rehabbing."

A lane appears from nowhere, rising out of a grove of trees. Suddenly, the camp is spread out before us—green hills, flags and banners, log structures. The bright blue of a lake sparkles beyond, racks of colorful canoes and kayaks lining the beach.

It's a dream only half an hour from Denver.

The tension in my chest relaxes as I take in our surroundings.

"This is amazing!" I gush.

We're barely out of the car when a smiling woman with an athletic build and graying hair comes to greet us.

"You must be Nova. I'm Robin, director of the camp." She shakes my hand before turning to the man at my side. "Hello, you."

Robin embraces Clay, and I'm surprised to see he lets her.

"I'll keep myself busy. I'll catch you back here in an hour or so." Clay shoves both hands in his pockets and heads toward another set of buildings.

"Thank you for your time, especially on short notice," I say.

I expand on what I told her on the phone, explain what Harlan's trying to do and that I'd like to ask a few questions to improve the plan.

"Why don't we start with a quick tour?"

"I'd love that."

We take the lane up to the main building, a huge log cabin. Inside, we walk the perimeter of the building while she answers one question after another. I take a few notes on my phone, but mostly I know I'll remember.

"It's a beautiful facility."

She points along the lake. "There are the campers' cabins. They're full in the summer, but at the moment, we have weekend and after-school programming." She gestures around us. "We're in the administration building now. We're working on a new art room."

I straighten. "Could I see it?"

"Of course."

Robin shows me into the next building, a stunning A-frame with windows everywhere. The end of the building is dedicated to a sprawling, vaulted room with huge tables and easels and paints. Sunshine spills into every corner.

"The light is so cool here. What kind of art do the kids do?"

"All kinds. Their latest thing is making bear masks." She shows me a collection of papier-mâché laid out along a table to dry. "You into art?"

"I was," I admit. "I got admitted to art school, but I never graduated."

"You can always return to it. I was working as a lawyer before I found myself here. I don't regret my time practicing, but running this program? It's a dream come true.

"I used to believe that we're supposed to find our

path. It took time to realize life is full of paths, like a tree branching out with thousands of possibilities. Unlike a tree, we can go back and choose another path. Life is full of second chances."

Her philosophy is energizing.

I ask her some more questions about things to keep in mind when setting up a program from scratch, what she'd do differently, and make notes for Harlan.

As we finish our conversation, I glance out the window at where the kids are gathered around a basketball court.

The pavement is freshly painted, the court surrounded by chain link fence. It looks new except for the net that hangs haphazardly off the hoop.

"Nothing stays picture perfect around here. We replaced it last week, but the kids have been swinging on it," Robin says. She's amused, not upset that the perfect image is tarnished.

Clay is at the center of the crowd, standing head and shoulders above the rest.

His shirt is tucked into the back of his shorts, his body muscled and glistening in the warm fall day.

He's good with them. For all that he makes himself out to be a bad mentor, a bad teammate, I can see him listening to those kids.

"Let's go watch before you break your neck," Robin says dryly.

I flush, caught out.

She grins, and we head outside together.

"He said he came here when he was injured?" I ask.

She nods. "But he doesn't advertise it. A lot of people would like to use this to build their brand, but he prefers to connect with the kids without media attention. Clay gets a lot of attention, good and bad. It's hard to live under that much pressure."

Clay pulls aside a kid who's on the sidelines and asks him a question. The boy answers, and Clay nods, then motions him closer. They practice a minute, and the boy breaks into a grin.

"They adore him," Robin murmurs.

And he adores them. He'd probably give me hell if I accused him of it though.

Robin steps forward, clapping her hands and making everyone look over. "Okay, we should let Clayton get back to his activities."

The kids groan, and Clay catches my eye. I swear his expression brightens a little.

I've been thinking of him nonstop since the barbeque. His words have been echoing through my mind.

"Wear mine. The next time you wear a jersey, you fucking wear mine."

Nothing has happened between us, not really, but I can't stop thinking about it.

Every second we're close, my skin is on fire. Every time I get a text from him, I bite my lip. I'm in a constant state of arousal, ready to explode at a gruff innuendo or an accidental touch.

Clay heads for me and Robin. "How're the new cabins?"

"Nearly finished," she says. "You're welcome to check them out."

Robin excuses herself to head back to the administration building.

"You're sweating," I tease when it's the two of us.

"You've never had a workout until you've chased around a bunch of ten-year-olds," he says wryly. "That's why we're going swimming."

He doesn't look gross—he looks sexy.

"Will it be refreshingly cold or skin-numbingly cold?" I ask.

Clay grins. "You can take it."

I'm not ready to back down from a challenge.

He takes me to the changerooms by the lake, where I put on the swimsuit he told me to bring.

It's a white two-piece with pink hearts on it that hugs my breasts and hips tighter than I remember. I threw it in my bag to come to Denver on a whim, and it's not especially lake worthy.

When I leave the building, his gaze skims over me from toes to lips.

A little shiver of anticipation runs through me.

I'm suddenly glad I brought these utterly insufficient scraps of fabric.

"Something wrong?" I ask.

"Not even a little," he says, his mouth curving at the corner.

The water *is* cold, but his closeness helps.

"You were amazing with them," I say once we're in.

We wade out to a wooden float a dozen or so yards out, where it's deep enough for me to barely touch. The water hits Clay in the chest.

"It's easy with kids. Adults have damage. I went to camp for the first time when I was twelve. It'd been a rough couple years, but I found somewhere I fit in. I was awkward. Always too big. Suddenly, I was celebrated for it."

I lift my knees, treading water.

"The kids are so full of joy. I'd love to draw out here sometime."

"Thought you only drew me," he huffs.

I roll my eyes. "I draw you plenty."

We share a half smile.

"Camp was the best time of my life. Sometime later when the stress gets to you, it stops being a game." He swims closer, water dripping off his lips. "I need to be right this year. I only have so many chances."

"At what? Your life?" My feet brush the sandy bottom of the lake.

"My life is on the court."

"Then who did I meet on the plane? Because I didn't know he played basketball. Or had messed up his knee. Or any of the other baggage. And I liked him."

His eyes glint.

He loops an arm around my waist under the water and pulls me closer.

Clay's thumbs stroke down my sides, slow and intentional, and my breath sticks in my throat.

"You cold?" he asks.

I shake my head and wrap my arms around his neck, vaguely aware there could be kids nearby.

He runs a hand up my arm, making me shiver from anticipation instead of chill. The entire time, his eyes don't leave mine.

He palms my back, his touch feeling so damn good.

"You believe in people," he murmurs.

I smile, my head lilting to one side. "You could try it sometime."

"It didn't work out."

My fingers trace the lines on his chest.

"Then try again," I whisper.

I didn't mean he should try with me.

Except... I want that. I want him to trust me, to let me in, even if he's not looking for someone to share his life with and I'm not sticking around.

His eyes darken. They're deeper than the lake,

than the entire ocean. He smells like salt and the forest that surrounds the camp, sharp and male and real.

I'm adrift in the water and his arms, living for the places his skin brushes mine.

We're not close enough.

The sound of hollering enters my brain moments before a group of campers comes up over the rise, clad in colorful T-shirts.

"Clay..." I whisper, ready to point out the interruption.

"Take a breath."

What...?

He drags me under the water, holding us both down. Pulls me closer, his hand threading into my hair at my nape.

His lips brush mine.

Just like that, he's kissing me. He's wild and insistent, hot and hard and nearly out of control.

He holds my head in place—he's not trying to be gentle. His other hand grips my ass and makes me grind against his ridged abs.

The water buoys us up, transports us to another plane where there's no up or down, where there's only him.

I can't breathe.

I don't need oxygen.

All I need is his huge body surrounding me, the heat of his mouth, the urgency of his hands.

I'm shivering, but I'm not cold.

It's so good. So much more than I imagined it could be.

My chest aches to fill with new air, my lungs burning with the want for him, for even more than just this.

The light splinters through the water, dancing on his tattoos, on the ink that envelopes him like a second skin and proves that he is everything I thought he was: hard and soft, dominant and gentle, powerful and vulnerable, beautiful and real...

He lets me break the surface.

"We better get out of here," he says as he pants, "or I'm going to do something very inappropriate."

I grin, and his eyes crinkle, too.

We get out and dry off, and it's as if he's lightened up since we took that swim.

"Robin said we could see one of the new cabins before we go."

He's up to something. "Okay."

I barely have time to slip on my sandals before he grabs my hand and tugs me to one of the little log outbuildings.

I pause in the cabin doorway. The modest room is equipped to sleep four, with two dressers and a full-length mirror. I cross to the bunk beds. "I loved these things as a kid."

These ones are a heavy wood, and fragrant. Oak maybe.

I climb up the ladder and drop onto the mattress, which is bare except for a fitted sheet.

Clay closes the door behind him, then pulls himself up next to me.

I gasp as the frame creaks from our combined weight. "We're going to break these."

"I'll replace 'em." He shifts over me, his huge body blocking out most of the light from the square window opposite.

My shirt slides up my stomach, and he lifts a tiny stone from my belly button. "Souvenir."

I laugh. "Trust me, I'm remembering today."

I loved watching him with those kids.

"You're a good teacher when you're patient," I add.

Clay's brows pull together. "You're saying I'm not normally."

I squint at him. "Not so much."

His lips curve up, and every time they do, I'm pulled in a little more by him.

I love seeing him like this. Playful and sexy. It's out of character, and I could happily pass out under the attention of those eyes, that smile.

He brushes my stomach with his thumb, a slow stroke that lights up every part of me. I suck in a breath and arch my back.

"You like pushing my buttons, Pink," he remarks, his eyes glinting with humor. "I'll push back."

The nickname makes me flush even before his

fingertips trail along the side of my ribs and up to my shoulder.

Heat pools between my thighs, and the sensation of being touched in all the right places takes over.

"Is that what that was back there?" I nod toward the lake. "Pushing back?"

His fingers thread into my damp hair, twisting and reminding me how his mouth felt on mine.

"It was me doing what I've been thinking about for a long damned time."

Hot, aching desire ripples through my stomach. I forgot how good it felt to have him touch me, to kiss me, the way everything in my body turns to liquid when he's near.

I'm supposed to be making good life decisions. Responsible ones.

But in some ways, this month is an escape from that responsibility. I'm working towards it, will start in earnest when I get back.

I want him.

So much.

"Tell me what you're thinking now," I whisper.

His face hardens, his jaw clenching. "You. I've tried not to. Since the barbeque, since the night in my car. But every time I think I can get your sweetness out of my head, there you are. I want to shake you until you see the world isn't as good as you pretend. I want to crawl inside you until I believe what you believe."

My breath catches.

"But right now," he goes on, "I want to strip you out of this poor excuse for a bikini and make you so thoroughly mine you'd rather burn Miles' jersey than wear it because you can't imagine anyone else's name on your skin."

19

NOVA

His words leave me throbbing.

I need him, even if it's wrong.

How can it be wrong when it feels so good?

A shiver of anticipation runs through me.

"Do it," I whisper.

His lips claim mine, rough and a little agitated. Our bodies are still cool from the lake, but a fire burns inside us. My fingers thread into his hair, pulling him down so I can press my lips to his.

It's on.

Me.

Clay.

A twin bunk bed.

The sound of campers outside.

Who is this girl? I have no idea.

He groans against my throat.

"I think about this every second," he says.

"Are we in the top or the bottom bunk when you think about it?"

He chuckles against my skin. "We're everywhere."

He reaches for the back of my bathing suit top, unclipping it deftly. Clay's head bumps the bunk overhead.

I want him so badly I can't remember a time before I wanted him.

"The Kodiaks' all-star is going to have a concussion, and it'll be my fault," I say.

He grins as he drags the top down my arms and tosses it behind him. "Worth it."

Clay's attention burns a hot trail from my face down my body, lingering on my breasts before returning. His eyes are dark with intent and approval.

"You're so beautiful," he says.

The way his gaze runs over me is like I'm in the Victoria Secret fashion show with wings sticking out from my back.

My nipples grow hard as his fingers tease along my ribs before cupping the swells of my breasts.

I arch my back, pressing myself into his touch.

He's already shirtless, and my fingers run over the smooth expanse of his skin, the expanse covered in tattoos. He's living art. I could look at him every day and never get enough.

I run my fingers over the ridges of his chest and abdomen. "You use these muscles for... cutting?

Guarding?" I try to remember the words Brooke told me at the game.

His lips twitch, but he pushes me onto my back, pinning my wrists above my head.

"I've never hooked up with someone who didn't care I'm a basketball player," he says. "I like it."

My gaze snaps to his to find Clay's warm eyes full of appreciation.

"I'm gonna show you how much."

His body is wide, muscular, a living sculpture carved from stone. The stark ridges of his abs run to either side of his navel and disappear into the waistband of his shorts.

When my attention continues downward, I swallow a gasp.

His erection is a huge, thick outline under his shorts.

It can't be that big.

There's no actual way he carries that around all day, not to mention that it would fit inside me.

I feel like I should have heavy equipment training to even touch what's between us.

He rolls to his side to graze my collarbone with kisses. I moan as he skims over my breasts and then circles my nipples with the tip of his tongue. His hands are huge, but they're gentle.

He works his way down my body, pausing over my navel to blow on it softly, making me laugh out loud. I'm still wet from the lake, but he makes sure every inch of my skin is warm and covered in his touch.

We don't fit in this bed. He doesn't seem concerned.

His fingers hook into the sides of my bikini bottoms. His warm hands press into the flesh of my hips, reaching around to the small of my lower back to tug me forward.

The heat from his palms burns through the fabric of my bathing suit.

He nudges at my thighs until they part, and he slips between them, his hard body against mine.

He presses a kiss to my temple, holding himself there briefly before moving down toward my mouth.

His breath is on my skin when, finally, he speaks again.

"I almost kept you underwater. But I want to find out if you taste as sweet as you look. I remember thinking with your pink hair, you'd taste like cotton candy."

Holy.

Every thought evaporates. All that's left is a throbbing need.

The need to be seen and touched. The need to be safe from judgment, like I am with him. Only with him.

Clay takes his time drawing the wet fabric down my hips. It sticks to my skin, making me squirm as he drags it down past my knees and ankles.

My body feels heavy and languid and warm, like molasses sliding through summer heat.

Suddenly, I'm naked in this bunk bed. There's nothing between us except want and need, and it's overwhelming.

He rocks back to look at me, inhaling sharply. "Fuck, Nova. You know I'm gonna think of you like this all the time now."

The words light me up, sending little spirals of pleasure through me.

I could say the same for him. His body is a work of art, and that's before the tattoos. Miles of tanned skin, smooth and rippling.

When I hone in on the bulge in his shorts again, there's a thrill of excitement blending with the fear.

He spreads my legs wide, and I shut my eyes tight at the sensation of his breath along my sensitive skin.

He runs a finger along the inside edge of my thigh, millimeters from where I'm wet and needy.

Nerves lace through me, and my toes flex.

Damn. His mouth is dangerous enough when we're talking.

The idea of him using his lips, his tongue, to—

"Nova."

I blink my eyes open to see him staring down at me. His expression is a mask of concerned intensity.

"What's wrong?"

Shit. Was it that obvious?

Of course I went and made the hottest moment of my life awkward.

"I just haven't done this a lot," I say, but it comes out more like a mumble.

He glances toward the window, then back at me. "How much is 'a lot'?"

Oh God. This is not how I wanted this to go.

Normally, he's good at making me feel like there's not five years of adult life experience between us. Right now, though, it's painfully obvious.

"A couple of guys, Brad, and... You know what? Never mind. I shouldn't have said that."

"I don't need names, Pink. I want to know why you went stiff on me."

Clay seems genuinely intent on knowing, so I give him the most honest answer I can.

"I was just thinking how every guy I've been with turned out to be an asshole, but it was nothing like this with them," I rush on as his expression darkens. "It didn't feel like this. You make me feel so good I can hardly stand it."

He stills.

"Give me your fingers," he says.

I do, and he takes them in his mouth, swirls his tongue around them. It's sensual and filthy, the way he sucks with his eyes on mine, and I could watch him do it all day.

Until he releases them with a pop.

He spreads my thighs again and waits.

"Oh, no, that's not happening," I say.

There's no way I'm getting myself off while he watches. He might think it's considerate, but it dials up the performance pressure another level because I literally am performing—for him.

"Because you don't want to, or because you're afraid?" he asks.

I watch him over me like an animal about to pounce on its prey. He's so big and intimidating and powerful, even like this.

He must see something on my face because he shifts up my body so that his hips are cradled between mine. My thighs spread even wider, as if they have a mind of their own, which they might as well because I am now putty in his hands.

"Don't think about me. Touch yourself," he murmurs against my mouth.

"I can't," I whisper.

"Yeah, you can. I bet you're good at it, too."

Between his words and his lips, breathing is impossible.

"I'll wait," he goes on between kisses. "But I can feel how bad you want it. And pretty soon, you won't be able to hold out."

I brush my fingers over my clit, and my hips snap up.

His groan of encouragement lights me up. "That's it. Good girl."

My shower fantasy rises up, only it's so much hotter in person.

He grips my hip, his thumb pressing next to my hipbone while his fingers dig into the flesh of my ass.

I give in to the sensations coursing through me and arch against the hand—my hand—between my legs.

Any self-consciousness slips away at the delicious pleasure of it, the way he growls his approval when I moan into the silent room.

"That's it, Pink."

I twist my face against the pillow. It's too much. It's everything.

"Need a taste." He grabs my hand and sucks my fingers into his mouth. "Knew it. Cotton candy."

Shit.

He's so hot, but more than that, he makes me feel hot.

Like when he guides my left index finger back into my core, as if he can't stand that I'm empty for another second.

I gasp as I am pushed all the way in, my knuckles bumping my entrance.

"Clay," I whisper, but the word is cut off by another moan as he slides another finger inside. I am full and tingling, and I've never felt like this before.

"Fuck me, you're beautiful." His murmured praise against my hip bone sends a shiver down my spine.

He works my fingers in and out of me, the heel of my hand grinding against my clit.

My hips tilt and roll as my fingers hit the little spots inside me that make me moan.

"Harder," I say because my whole body is arching, twisting, and burning for more.

His eyes squeeze shut as he brings my fingers in hard and fast.

"I'm so close."

My fingers are working me, he's working me, and it feels like we're creating something incredible together.

He drags me down the bed, grabs my other wrist and pins it flat against the sheets.

A tremor racks my body.

"More?"

I nod.

He slides back, taking my fingers from me, and I want to cry in protest. I thrust up my hips, trying to catch both our hands, but he pulls away. "Don't come yet," he orders, his eyes searching mine for confirmation that I will obey him.

"Why not?" I breathe out a laugh at the absurdity of his command.

"Because I like watching you too much."

His thumb presses against my hip bone, matching the force of his words.

I gasp. My orgasm is already there in the pit of my stomach.

"Nova..." he warns.

I can't help it. I feel too good, and he's too hot, and I'm too turned on.

He must know what I'm feeling because with a curse, he plunges my fingers back inside me.

I'm needy and full and desperate. I squeeze my eyes closed, but I still feel his attention on me.

"Come, Pink," he murmurs. "Come all over your fingers so I can lick it off."

His thumb rubs across my clit, and I cry out from the pressure.

I fall over the edge, waves of pleasure racking my body.

Every ounce of feeling is amplified by his presence, his arousal, like I'm coming for both of us.

I can't move. It was too much. It was too good.

When I finish, I push up onto my elbows to see him watching me, his expression reverent from the pleasure he seems to take from watching me come undone.

He takes my fingers and sucks them into his mouth. It's outrageously sexy and surprisingly sweet at once. "That was the hottest thing I've ever seen."

I flush with pleasure.

Noise outside drags me back to where we are.

He notices, too.

We scramble out of bed, him moving gracefully and me tripping.

He tosses me my shorts, then tugs on his own.

I work them up my hips. "Ever?" I prompt.

"Mhmm."

I arch my back, grinning as his gaze lands on my breasts.

"Sexier than Kodashians sending you naked pictures?"

"By a long shot."

There's no time. I grab for my bag and drag a T-shirt on.

"I like knowing I'm good at something," I say. "I want to tell the world."

"Tell the world about your other skills. Not this one," he warns, pocketing my bikini top.

We run for it, tripping over one another.

"Why? You want to keep me for yourself?" I tease.

When I reach for the door, his hand covers mine.

Clay grabs my neck from behind and pulls me back against him, tipping my chin up for a hard kiss that feels as good as the orgasm.

I'm breathless when he pulls back.

"Yeah, I fucking might."

20

NOVA

"You're filthy."

Mari's voice tears into my thoughts, and I snap my head up. "Excuse me?"

My sister crosses the solarium to where I'm bent over my sketchpad.

I close the cover as casually as possible as she reaches for a piece of my hair, pulling out a leaf. "What were you up to all day?"

"Secret mission." I showered when I got home from the camp but didn't do my hair. My breath sticks in my chest as she scrutinizes my appearance.

I want to tell her about Clay because she's my sister and sharing these feelings seems right, but we're still getting back on good terms. I just got out of a yearlong relationship with Brad. Hooking up with my future brother-in-law's grumpy all-star doesn't seem like the way to demonstrate sound judgment.

"How was work?" I ask instead.

Mari makes a face and kicks off her heels, sitting on the window seat opposite me. Her feet brush mine. "My boss brought in a new campaign for a huge client. I want to direct it, but two of us are competing."

"Tell her you could do it better. She promoted you. This is your chance to remind her why. And if that fails," I go on, "the bachelorette is this weekend. Massages and relaxation."

She nods slowly.

"You're right. What are you drawing?"

I hold out the sketchpad.

On the page is a drawing of the altar, plus the back of Mari's dress.

My sister's mouth parts softly. "This is beautiful, Nova. I love these flowers." She gestures to the ones draped across the altar.

"They're ranunculus. Like roses but rounder, tighter. Kind of squished looking." I mimic their shape with my hands.

"I'm still figuring out how to replace the roses I wanted. They'd be perfect."

We share a smile.

"I remember when you got into art school," she says after a moment. "You were so excited. Do you wish you'd stayed?"

"Sometimes."

"But you've kept drawing all this time."

"A little. More recently." It feels good. I feel like part of myself I'd buried is waking up.

"What changed?" Mari asks.

"You want to keep me for yourself?"

"I fucking might."

Seeing him with the kids at the camp made me realize what a good guy he is, even if he doesn't see himself that way. I want him to be that version of himself. I want to watch him do it. And I want the way he makes me feel when we're alone, when his eyes turn black and he whispers dirty things in my ear.

I can't tell my sister about Clay. She's finally looking at me as though she sees me just a little.

"I guess I realized I wasn't feeling like myself. I feel the most at home when I'm drawing."

She doesn't nod but seems to understand. "I need to show these flowers to the florist. Can I have this?"

"Of course." I carefully tear the sheet out of my sketchbook and hand it to her.

Her shoulders round happily as she takes it in. "Do you want to grab dinner later? There's an Italian place with the most amazing wine list."

It's the first time since I've been here that my sister has suggested dinner just the two of us.

I shove down any thoughts of a confession. "I'd love to."

"Are you sure you have time to pick them up this morning?" Chloe asks over the phone.

"No problem!" I say into the hands-free of the Volvo.

The day of the bachelorette party might be calling for rain, but we're heading to a spa for a full day of pampering.

It was my idea to order custom cupcakes, and when they're assembled, they'll form the shape of Mari's dress. It's a detail I hope she'll love.

"Hi. Cupcakes for Mari?" I ask the woman at the bakery when I arrive, and she looks at me.

She's on the phone and nods to a covered slab-cake plate.

I take a peek because I want them to be perfect.

They're gorgeous.

I pay for them and carefully carry them back to the car.

When I get there, a message from Clay comes in.

Grumpy Baller: What're you doing today?

Nova: Getting naked with a bunch of women.

Grumpy Baller: Pics or it didn't happen.

I grin.

Nova: It's Mari's bachelorette. I'm picking up cupcakes, then we're going to the spa.

Grumpy Baller: She's lucky to have you.

His words put a little extra bounce in my step as I head to the Four Seasons.

He's been away the last few days playing a road game I watched on Harlan and Mari's huge TV last night. It was strange hearing the commentators talk about him like he's famous, but he is.

When the Kodiaks won, I was jumping up and down enough to spill popcorn everywhere.

I texted him after to say congrats, not expecting a response.

One came back almost immediately.

Grumpy Baller: Thanks Pink. Wish you were here to see it.

Today there are six of us: me, Chloe, Brooke, Mari, and two other friends of Mari's I haven't met.

The spa attendants get us checked in and get us off to our first appointments.

The massages fly by in a wave of pleasure, plus a few moans when the technician hits an especially tight spot. We arranged for Mari to get an extra body treatment to help her relax while the rest of us get manicures and pedicures.

Chloe insisted on picking up the bill even though I protested.

I haven't felt this pampered in forever. Maybe it's the altitude taking, but I didn't realize how much stress had accumulated in my body between work and Brad.

By the time we all reconvene in our robes, we're two bottles of champagne in. We open a third for Mari.

She takes it, beaming, and we do a toast.

"One more thing!" I leap up, the separators still between my toes, and stumble toward the table in the corner.

I unveil the cupcakes, and the girls ooh and ahh.

"They're beautiful."

"And vegan," I say proudly.

Mari wrinkles her nose. "I can't eat that before my wedding."

"It's ten days, Mar. And they're mini cupcakes."

Grudgingly, she takes one and pops it into her mouth.

"That's good," she admits, washing it down with champagne. "I haven't been eating carbs for six months."

She reaches for another.

"Are you and Harlan excited for the honeymoon?

Nothing but each other for two entire weeks," Chloe says.

Mari smiles. "We haven't had that much time alone together despite living under the same roof. We're always working."

"Now you don't even have to get dressed," Brooke points out between sips.

We all laugh.

"Will the team survive without him?" Mari asks Chloe.

"They'll be fine."

She nods. "I don't want to be the one responsible for problems his first year."

"Mar, he has a life," I point out, reaching for a cupcake.

She turns it over. "Maybe you're right."

We go back to gossiping, and thirty minutes later, she's flushed.

"Everything okay?" I ask as she rises, frowning.

"Yes, I need to use the bathroom."

She sways a little.

"Let me help. That champagne is deadly." I follow her, holding her arm.

I'm waiting outside the stalls for a few minutes before I hear groaning.

"Mar? You okay?"

"I don't feel well."

"What did you eat besides champagne?"

"Nothing today except the cupcakes."

"Maybe you should have had breakfast."

"I never have breakfast."

There's another groan.

I scoot back out to the other girls. "Um, don't freak out, but did anyone else feel weird after the cupcakes?"

Heads shake.

"It was the best buttercream icing I've ever had," Brooke says.

"No, those were vegan. No butter, no eggs," I insist.

She stares me down.

"Shit."

I dash back to the washrooms, stopping by the lockers to fish around in my bag for the receipt. Sure enough, it says vegan, but the evidence is to the contrary.

"Mar, the cupcakes might have been slightly less vegan than we thought."

The growl from inside the stall makes me wince.

The toilet flushes, and my sister emerges, bent over.

Chloe appears in the doorway, a bottle in one hand and a glass of water in the other.

"Hey, hon, I have pills. My emergency stash. Two of the players are lactose intolerant, and it makes for a bad media day if they're uncomfortable."

She passes my sister the pills and glass, and Mari chugs it gratefully. "Thank God."

"They might not fix everything, but they'll help."

"What can I do?" I ask.

"You've done enough," Mari says.

Chloe sighs. "Why don't you go back and hang with the other girls? Tell them we'll be out in a few minutes."

I chew on my lip as my shoulders slump, and I head back outside to fill them in.

A few minutes later, Mari and Chloe appear.

"I'm going to have Harlan pick me up and take me home."

"I can drive you," I offer.

"No. It's fine." She looks at me.

Brooke grabs my shoulder. "You can crash at mine tonight if you want."

Because going home with a soon-to-be-bride who's sick because I fucked up is a bad idea, she means.

"Thanks."

I check my phone, miserable, and find a text from Clay.

Grumpy Baller: I'm still waiting on those pics.

Nova: It was a bust. I screwed everything up.

Grumpy Baller: I'm heading home from the gym. Let me pick you up.

Nova: What's your address? I'll come to you.

He tells me, and I take an Uber there, feeling equal parts dejected and tipsy.

The building is a modern high-rise, full of glass with big, landscaped balconies.

The elevator ride seems to take forever.

When I get to his floor and knock, he opens the door looking handsome in a gray Henley that pulls across his muscles and is shoved up his arms.

His hair is still damp from a shower. One of his pant legs is shoved up to his thigh, and there's an ice pack strapped to his knee.

For a moment, it's possible the world isn't ending, because he's standing here.

I hold out a cupcake.

"Are you lactose intolerant?" I ask in a small voice.

"Fuck no." He takes the cupcake in one hand and grabs my forearm with the other. "Now get your ass in here."

I feel a bit better already.

Clay shows me around his place.

The apartment is spacious, with a lofted ceiling and huge windows with a view of the city. The kitchen is sleek and modern, cabinets painted white and black. The furniture is clean and polished, like he's not living there but staging his own place. There are faint hints of lemon and lime mixed with a warm masculine scent that I breathe in deep.

"This is the guest bedroom." Partway down the hall, he gestures to a bedroom larger than mine back in Boston. The walls are lined with shelves containing trophies and plaques and banners.

"Holy." I cut him a look. "These are all for basketball?"

"I am pretty great at it."

The laughter that bubbles up feels good.

He continues the tour, and I take one more look at all the gold before following.

"And this…" He hits the light switch at the end of the hall. "Is me."

The main bedroom is huge. An expanse of cream carpet, matching walls, a seating area at one end, plus a king bed that seems to go on forever.

It hits me.

Is this why he invited me over?

Probably.

I've fantasized about having sex with him more times than I care to count, but I didn't imagine it happening like this.

Although now that I'm looking up at him, his eyes darkening by the second, I know we could make it work.

My fingers reach for the buttons on my top, and he frowns.

Clay takes my hand, stopping me.

"Oh. I thought you wanted to..." I trail off.

Clearly, I misread this. I've managed to humiliate myself twice today.

"I really fucking want to, Nova. But not tonight. Not when you're beating yourself up over something you didn't do."

Up close, I can count the flecks of gold in his dark eyes. It feels like he's willing me to understand.

I do, and I'm grateful.

I sigh out a little breath of relief as he tugs me back toward the living room.

He sinks into the huge L-shaped couch, and I follow his lead. He removes the ice pack from his knee and sets it on the coffee table. Then, to my surprise, he draws me between his legs and pulls my back to his front.

"So, tell me what happened at this party." Clay's voice vibrates along my skin.

I fill him in, one sordid detail at a time while trying to ignore the fact that I'm nestled against his hard, warm body. It's easier that I don't have to look at his expression.

Except by the end, his chest is rocking with laughter.

I spin to face him.

"It's not funny!" I protest, hitting him in the stomach. My hand bounces easily off his ridged abs.

"It's kind of funny. Got any more of those cupcakes?"

I roll my eyes, but my lips twitch.

"Mari probably had them burned. Even though I double-checked, triple-checked... something went wrong, and I screwed up, and Chloe saved the day. Mari's always been the perfect one, the responsible one, the one with everything together."

"I don't believe that."

"It's true."

Clay listens, his eyes dark and intent as I tell him about us growing up together.

"I never minded being on the road. She hated it. Hated leaving friends, leaving places. Our parents were really kind people, and they cared about us, but Mari had a harder time with the change than I did. Now that we're grown, Mari's found an anchor—in her work and this place and Harlan. Me? I'm a balloon floating around not sure how to find the ground."

I sigh in his arms.

"My mom used to sing this song, 'Home.' It was the only time Mari would curl up next to Mom, that it seemed like they understood one another. I have a recording of her singing it. I'm trying to find it for the wedding."

"I'm sure she'll love it."

I nod, swallowing as my fingers twist together and unlace.

"I have some friends, but she's my family. The one who has to love me no matter what, who knows I'll always love her." I take a shallow breath. "When my parents died, they were on vacation in Costa Rica. Mari was busy working, but I was in my first year of art school. I was supposed to go with them but flaked at the last minute and bailed because of things I wanted to do at school. I told them to take this plane tour for me, and they did. Only the weather was bad, and they crashed."

Guilt and grief rise up, consuming me until my lungs burn and my ribs threaten to crack.

"Their deaths weren't your fault," he murmurs.

"I should have been with them," I insist. "I should have been on that plane."

Clay takes my face in his hands and swipes at my cheeks, at the tears I didn't notice before now.

"I'm fucking glad you weren't," he whispers against my lips.

His expression makes the guilt in my chest ease, replacing it with a feeling of warmth and hope.

"You are?" I blink up at him. It's the first time someone's said that to me, and it means the world.

"Fuck yes. For starters"—he pulls back an inch—"no one would've been on that commercial flight last month to tell me I should consider a career in basketball. And you see how well that worked out."

My eyes squeeze shut. "Stop it—"

His laugher rumbles through me, and he pulls me tight until we're both rocking with it.

"Wanna watch a movie?"

"Yes."

He turns on the TV and flicks to an On Demand channel with every film known to man before handing me the remote.

"Anything I want?"

"Anything."

I choose *The Princess Bride*, which has an ill-fated wedding through no fault of the wedding party.

Before I fall asleep in Clay's arms, I decide the events of today were almost worth it because they gave me this moment.

21

NOVA

The next day, I'm at the stadium and working on a different set of drawings that have nothing to do with my sister's wedding.

Harlan said I could come and go as I wanted, and security made it easy. So, it wasn't difficult to plan my visit to match with the Kodiaks' on-court practice while Mari's at work.

Down on the court, the guys are in practice jerseys, running drills. I never before appreciated how tightly scripted the game is. Every act of aggression on the court, every defensive play, is planned and rehearsed over and over.

Right now, the coaches hold tablets, talking amongst themselves. The head coach watches intently, arms crossed as Clay brings the ball up the court, guarded closely by the rookie.

Clay spins away, beating the rookie by a full

second. There's a moment's hesitation when he shifts his weight.

Miles cuts toward the edge of the court and calls out. Clay's head snaps up, and he fires a pass to his teammate, who takes a three that's all net.

Jayden celebrates, high-fiving Clay, who looks as if he's up in his head about something. *The knee?*

Even still, I'm sitting up in the corporate box, high enough that none of the players will notice me. It's not that Clay wouldn't be okay with me showing up, but I'm not here to see him. Not entirely.

I watch, and I draw.

"Don't tell me you're changing horses mid-race." Brooke drops onto the seat next to me and makes me jump.

"How are you so quiet in heels?"

"Practice." She tosses her braids over a shoulder, then takes in the drawing I'm working on. "You hitting on my brother?"

"No." I flip the page to the previous one. "I have all the guys. Miles, too."

Her eyes narrow. She tugs the sketchbook into her lap, her lavender nails brushing the edges of the page. "Damn. You should put your work in galleries. I'm not just saying that. I don't bullshit. If they were ass, I'd tell you."

I laugh. "Thanks?"

I like having someone in my life who says what she means. Brooke is together and confident like my sister, but we don't have the same drama from years of rubbing against one another.

Brooke holds up the sketch of Miles mid-shot. "His mouth is wrong. It goes up right there when he's shooting a three."

I look between her and the guys, but his back is turned as they prep another play.

"How'd you know it's a three?"

"The legs. The concentration on his face. He always gets that dialed-in Jason Bourne look when he's trolling the arc."

"See something you like?"

Miles has caught us staring, and all the guys look up. Clay swipes his face with a towel, then his gaze meets mine. His chin lifts in a nod.

A secret nod.

A high-school hot guy nod.

A guy who made you come in a bunk bed and held you while you watched *The Princess Bride* nod.

I try to play it cool and pretend I'm not lit up by the fact that Clayton Wade, the sexiest man I've ever seen, the best player on an entire team of professional athletes, is staring at me as if I'm the only thing worth seeing.

I can't look away.

Just when I think I can contain the feelings, can keep myself from catching on fire...

Clay strips off his jersey.

Heat stokes between my thighs like a secret sin.

I know how those muscles feel against me. How he sounds, that low growl in my ear.

He knows I'm watching, and he likes it. He takes his time crossing to the side of the court to grab a new shirt.

If he walked up here and said he wanted to fuck me in front of everyone, it would take every ounce of my willpower not to lie down on the floor and let him do it.

Coach blows his whistle. "Back to work!"

They focus again in an instant. It takes me way longer.

Brooke passes the drawing back.

"Maybe you're right about the mouth," I say when I look at it again. "You know him suspiciously well."

"He's my brother's best friend. I've seen him every way there is."

We both watch the players for a moment.

I say, "By 'every way,' you mean…"

She folds her slim arms. "Don't."

"Why not? He's cute," I say. His wavy dark hair and the dimple when he grins. He's got a sense of humor and is a charming playboy.

"First, my brother would kill him. Then me. Then bring Miles back to life and kill him again."

I'm intrigued enough to close my sketchbook and set it on the next seat over.

Brooke's eyes are still on the court. "You can love

these guys, Nova, but they'll always love basketball more."

The decisiveness of her words takes me aback, but she continues.

"I think you're good for Clay. He's probably even good for you. But I want to be your friend, and friends tell each other what's up, and what's up is that you won't be the love of his life. He already has one."

I turn that over. "I don't want to come between him and basketball. I want to love something like they love basketball."

I expect Brooke to call me naïve or silly, but she only laughs.

"Have a good time. Bang him until you can't walk. Hell, until neither of you can." She shoots me an arch look. "And if it ends badly, I'm here."

The team takes a break, and Clay goes for his phone.

Mine's buzzing a moment later.

Grumpy Baller: Got you tickets for our next preseason game.

He sends through an image of a VIP pass.

Nova: That's in LA.

Grumpy Baller: You deserve better than

watching on TV.

Grumpy Baller: I promise I'll be better behaved after. As long as you wear my jersey.

I want to go. So badly. But it means a flight, which I hate.

Plus, it's a week until the wedding, and even though everything is on track, there's no reason I can think of to justify this getaway to my sister.

"You going to the LA game?" I ask Brooke.

"Wasn't planning on it."

Brooke looks over my shoulder, then clears her throat.

"There's a brand I've been meaning to meet in LA. I could see them while I'm there. We could catch a ride together."

My breath catches. "Really?"

"Sure." Brooke taps a polished nail against her lips. "Maybe I need help on this trip."

I throw my arms around her neck, and she hugs me back.

"It'll be a train wreck," she mumbles into my neck.

I pull back and frown. "Why?"

"LA is the best. They've won the last two years. If you think the first two games were intense, you have no idea what you're in for."

22

CLAY

*E*xhibition games don't count for anything on paper. They're about pride. Momentum. Your first chance to check how your off-season work is coming together. Playing against the best team in the league is like reading the tea leaves on your chances to win this year.

There's also the fact that the guys on the other side of the court could be my teammates. But today, that doesn't matter. I'm in a Denver uniform, and that's where my allegiance lies for the full forty-eight minutes of game clock.

"Bring it in, boys," says Coach. "After the last game, there'll be attention on Clay. Remember to rotate on defense. Keep the screen and roll open. Kodiaks on three."

Everyone's hands go in, then up.

I turn toward the court and lock eyes with the opposing point guard.

The cheering of the LA fans fades into the background. The stands are full of fans in LA colors, interspersed with a few brave standouts of ours.

I catch sight of Nova, and adrenaline surges through me that has nothing to do with the game.

I make millions playing basketball.

I'd touch her every night for free.

She looks cute as hell in a black leather jacket, her pink hair flying as she bounces up and down, but it's not the jersey I sent her as part of a gift basket I instructed to have waiting on her plane.

She's not ready to announce her feelings.

What are her feelings?

Having her come to my place, fall asleep on my couch until I extricated myself and tucked her in—all of it felt more intimate than anything I've done in a long time.

None of it matters right now, I remind myself as the whistle blows.

It's impossible to know how they've game-planned for us, but when the ball goes up, Atlas takes the tip for the team, and LA's plan becomes clear pretty quickly.

Jayden takes it down the court, then over to me. I blast through their defense and score to deafening applause.

They take it back the other way, slicing through our guys like I did theirs.

The next time, Jay looks for Rookie. He shakes loose his defender and grabs the pass, cutting to the basket for a layup... and gets stripped by their center.

The crowd erupts.

For the next five minutes, it's a painful grind.

Coach doesn't make a change. What the hell? Rookie's playing badly. I would've subbed him out. But apparently Coach wants us to figure this out.

There's only one way out of this. The next time back our way, I nod to Jayden.

They're on me from the second my hands find the ball. Doubling me, making everything hard. I grind my teeth and plow through them to the basket for a layup, collecting a hard foul for my trouble.

When I go to the line, the first ball swishes through the net, and I shoot a look at the LA point guard.

The energy lights the competitive fire in me.

We claw back in the first quarter.

At halftime, we're up by four thanks to me carrying the team on my shoulders.

Coach pulls me aside in the locker room. "It's preseason. Let Rookie play."

"Do you want to win or not?"

He's making me look bad, which is bad for my trade value.

"It's a long season, Clay."

I close the distance between us. "You know LA. They smell blood in the water, they'll own us all year."

When we return for the second half, I look up and see Nova in the stands.

She came all this way to see me play. Got on a plane when I know how much that fucks her up.

Sure, she doesn't know I chartered the most comfortable plane I could get for under twenty people.

Still.

No matter what other things I'm feeling, I want to be better. For me and for her.

I try to take a back seat. I shake off Jayden and nod to Rookie. Then Rookie misses, and my frustration rises up.

I get open for Jayden, who passes to me.

A guy on the other team slams into me, and I go down hard.

"Try not to damage the merchandise." Their point guard holds out a hand to help me up.

His words have my heart thudding harder. He's the leader of the LA team. He'd be as likely to know what they're talking about as anyone.

I shake him off and wait for one of my teammates to help me up.

The next ten plays are similarly brutal.

I get the ball.

They trap me.

I fight through, dragging us back in the points.

It's painful to be part of, and I bet it's even more painful to watch.

Coach motions me over. "I got a play for you to run." He points at the bench.

I grab the neck of my jersey in my fist. "I'm the only one who can save this."

"There's a nice seat for you. Enjoy it until I've decided you're comfortable enough to get in the game again."

I stomp over to my seat.

The next quarter is dismal, interrupted only by the throbbing of my knee. I ignore it.

"Coach, put me in." I can fix this. I know it.

"No."

I grab my jersey and rip it clean in two.

∽

We lose by four.

Four fucking points.

I'm off the bench and the first one in the locker room before Coach can finish explaining plans for our team dinner.

In the shower, I turn the water to punishingly hot. *This is bullshit. There's no point in me riding the bench. I'm the top scorer on this team. All I want is to win.*

I grab my things and am halfway down the hall when I hear her voice.

"Clay?"

I turn back to see Nova, clutching the cord of her VIP badge.

"What happened out there?"

"We got our asses handed to us."

Her eyes glint. "It wasn't so bad."

"It was brutal because I could've fixed it. I don't like to lose."

"Then teach them how to win."

I exhale hard. I can't tell her LA is my endgame. I don't want to see the way she'd look at me if she knew my plan.

I feel the urge to push her away and bury my pain somewhere deep, to say she couldn't possibly understand.

But I don't want to push her away.

"I might not know much about basketball, Clay, but I hear it's a team sport."

I cock my head. "Oh yeah?"

"Mhmm." She smiles. "You don't need to take it all on. The wins or the losses."

She comes close, and I let her. I inhale the scent of her shampoo, tugging her body against mine. "Say that again."

Nova laughs and hugs me back. "It's not all about you."

It should feel horrible. Instead, there's relief.

Where the fuck was she when I was a kid?

"Can I show you something?" She pulls her sketchpad from her big bag and holds it out.

First Jay.

Then Miles.

Atlas.

Rookie.

I don't have words.

Not because they're good, though they are, but because she sees something in each of them that I've never even looked for.

"This one is my favorite." She turns the page to reveal one of me.

I'm fearless.

The kind of fearless that doesn't get threatened by the other team or his own.

My chest constricts. I want to be the man in this image. The man she sees.

I want to prove to ownership, to Harlan, to Coach, that I'm worth what they paid to get me here. Today, I wasn't.

I'm fascinated by the way she looks at me and obsessed with the possibility I could be that man now, again. I feel unburdened, and hopeful, and lighter than I have since college. Maybe even before then.

I look both ways down the hall, waiting for an LA staff person to pass before I drag Nova against me. She makes a little sound of surprise, as though she doesn't see how fucking inevitable it is.

I kiss her with the desperation and frustration left from the game, plus the desire that's been building in me since we visited the Kodiak Camp.

There's chemistry between us, but it's more than that. I find myself looking for her whether she's there or not. I need her sunshine in my day. I want to make hers better, too.

And yeah, every time I've jerked off the past two weeks, it's her face I've seen. I want to touch her, tease her, make her lose her mind with pleasure. I want to hear her moan my name when she comes, feel her tighten around my cock, to wrap her pink-blonde hair around my hand while I stroke into her over and over until she forgets every asshole who dared put his unworthy hands on her.

Her hands fall on my abs, lightly clinging through my clean shirt.

"What was that for?" she asks when I pull back, her expression dazed.

My thumbs slip beneath the waistband of her pants and rub circles over her hips. Her breath catches, her blue eyes turning the most fascinating shade of aqua.

"For being here."

"Someone made my flight easy thanks to tequila and eye masks."

"The least I could do." My lips twitch. "There's something I gotta do tonight. I want you to come with me."

She hesitates, tossing a look over her shoulder before looking back at me. "I'm eating with Brooke, plus you have team stuff."

I know there's risk in meeting, for both of us.

But I need her. Not some of her—all of her.

"Please."

23

NOVA

Brooke: You almost ready? I can be downstairs in ten.

I said I'd meet her for dinner, but the chance to spend tonight with Clay is beyond tempting.

Not because I'd get to be with him in LA for the evening, but because it seemed like he needed me.

I hit Brooke's contact.

"How much would you hate me if I bailed on dinner?" I ask when she answers on the first ring.

"So much. I'd complain about it all night to one of the super cute LA trainers who asked me out for drinks."

My lips curve.

"You sound tired. You should take a nap," she goes on. The humor in her voice is barely veiled.

"Maybe I should."

"Don't forget to wear the cute dress. For your nap."

I laugh.

"Hey, Brooke? Thank you. That means a lot." She's being exceedingly cool about me changing our plans, especially since she came to LA for me in the first place.

"No worries. I've got your back."

After we hang up, another text chimes.

Grumpy Baller: Meet you out front in an hour.

I go to my closet and pull out the dress I brought for tonight. It's short and silver with tiny straps, and the bottom hits mid-thigh. It's a little over the top, especially with the silver shoes Brooke gave me.

After the game, I showered and washed my hair, blow drying it straight before setting it in soft waves.

Now, I do my makeup—smoky eyes and nude lips.

The effect is pretty damn good. When I step into the dress and heels, I'm bubbling with nervous anticipation.

I grab my leather jacket and toss it on before sneaking a look at myself in the mirror. I look hot and sophisticated, but I still feel like me.

When I get down to the car, Clay looks up at me

from his phone, and his expression goes slack. "You're gorgeous."

The words are soft and edgy, like a curse muttered under his breath.

"You look good yourself." I take in the button-down shirt that clings to his muscled chest and shoulders, the dark pants hugging his hips.

He holds the back door of the limo for me, and I shift inside.

"Where are we going?"

"Dinner but I need to make a stop first." Clay takes up half the back seat of the limo. "I was watching you tonight in the stands."

"Oh, is that why we lost? I'll send Coach a fruit basket as an apology."

Clay chuckles, his entire chest rumbling.

"You looked like you guys were getting into it."

"We have different ideas about how to solve problems. Plus, Rookie should've been better."

"Will you talk to him about it?"

"He's got to figure some shit out on his own."

Clay pulls my back to his front, a strong arm around my ribs. Arousal dances in my stomach.

I think of Brooke's words about having fun.

I shift in my seat, crossing one leg over the other.

His touch skims down my side to my thigh, slipping toward the hem of my dress.

My breath catches as his fingers inch higher.

"Show me what's under here," he rasps.

"I got them for you."

I lift the edge of my skirt to reveal the thong I bought with the LA team's logo.

"You're fucking kidding me." His voice is strangled. "I told you there'd be consequences if you showed up wearing someone else's number again."

"There's no number on these," I say helpfully.

Clay buzzes up the panel between the seats.

"This drive just got longer."

The hairs on my neck lift as he wraps an arm around me and drags me over him, his front to my back.

Then he rips my underwear off and buzzes the window down, tossing them outside before I can protest.

"That was unnecessary," I say.

"It was entirely necessary," he murmurs against my neck.

He's like granite under me, the ridges of his stomach through his shirt and my dress. But it's his fingers playing with the soft skin at the inside of my thigh that make me pant.

Clay slides his hand between my legs, making a sound of approval.

"You're wet."

My head falls back against his shoulder.

He's so big and hard I can't even think of where I am, much less that there's a chauffeur in the front seat. I grind my ass against him, seeking relief, and he presses his mouth to the side of my neck, his stubble grazing my skin with a scrape of sensation.

"You've been wanting this all day, haven't you?"

"Mmm."

"Tell me who this is for."

He swipes a finger through my wetness, and I bite my lip to stop the groan.

"The limo," I whisper. "I get hot for a car with an L-couch for a back seat."

"The limo," he repeats. "You like the idea of being pushed into these leather seats. You want that sweet body teased until you make a sticky mess."

"Yes," I say, my head spinning.

"How about this finger?" He hooks a digit inside me with a soft stroke.

I gasp at the feel of him filling me. "I love that finger."

"That's my girl."

The limo drives a few more blocks, and Clay's breathing speeds up as he fingers me, my hand in his lap, coaxing him through his pants.

He's so hard.

He's going to fuck me.

I have to have him.

I reach for the button of his slacks.

He grabs my wrist, pinning it down at my side.

"Not yet."

I try to shake him off. "I want you."

"Not here."

He's huge and determined. My fingers dig into his arms as I arch my hips to ride the feeling.

I groan.

His thumb brushes my clit. "Tell me again who this is for."

I didn't realize how spun I've been the past few days without him.

His fingers withdraw, and I want to cry.

"It's for you."

His lips brush my ear. When he speaks, he's gentle and tortured at once. "Good girl. You think I haven't thought about taking you every way there is?"

He presses his fingers to my mouth, and I suck on them. I'm drunk on his words and my own taste.

"Every damn way." His fingers go back between my legs.

My clit swells as he rubs again, pumping his fingers in and out. My hips arch wildly, but he binds me against him, his arm like rope.

"This is what you asked for, Pink. Wearing another team's colors under your skirt."

It's more than I wanted. More than I can take.

"When you come on my fingers, you'll coat every inch of me." His voice is a dirty rasp. "So, there's no question who you're coming for."

There's no way I won't.

He slips a third finger inside me, and I'm so full and so wet I cry out.

His mouth sucks on my neck, his teeth dragging.

"You know how it feels to watch you walk around practice with your damn sketchbook, so fucking sweet, and imagine you dropping it so I can watch you pick it up? To see that perfect ass and imagine all I could do to it?"

He fucks me harder with his fingers. The sound of it fills the limo.

"Oh God."

It starts at my core. It's like I need to expand but can't because he's holding me so tightly, his fingers not letting up.

"Clay!" I bite my tongue to keep from screaming.

His voice is so deep and hoarse I barely recognize it. "Come for me, Nova."

The climax rips through my body in a wave.

I come so hard that the limo rocks.

It's so powerful I'm wrecked.

But he doesn't let up. He continues to rub my clit with his thumb. The pressure is almost too much as I'm still coming down.

I reach for his hand to make him stop, but he grabs my wrist and pins it behind my back. The car moves forward, and I'm lost again.

"I've wanted to watch you come since the first day I saw you." He's so close to my ear his words are a vibration that has me panting. "I've wanted to hear you scream my name."

He pushes two fingers back inside of me, and I mewl.

I'm at his mercy, and I love it.

He's taking me apart, leaving me with nothing to hold on to.

His lips brush my ear. "Again."

"I can't," I whimper.

"You can." He commands it. My head falls back against his shoulder again. My entire body is tight and hot.

"Come on, baby." Clay's breath is hot against my skin. "Come for me."

My hips rise as my stomach sinks, and a second orgasm rips through me.

It's so powerful, so intense, I can't hear anything but the ringing in my ears.

Only Clay and his demand that I give him everything.

Only the pulse of his fingers deep inside me.

The limo comes to a stop, and Clay pulls his fingers from me. He grabs a cloth napkin from the door and wipes his hands.

He gathers my hair off my neck and presses his mouth there. "Next time, it won't be my fingers. And that's a fucking promise."

I shiver as he helps smooth my hair back into place.

I don't realize the car has pulled to a stop until he holds out a hand.

"I get one every year. Mark the end of one season and the start of another," Clay says as I look up at the sign for Ink and Glory after he helps me out and I adjust my dress, my core still thrumming.

"Figured you see me so well that you could help me pick it out."

The idea that he'd include me in this floors me. He keeps his cards close, and the ink on his body is as close to a tapestry of his feelings as anything you're likely to find.

My heart swells. "I'd love to."

We look at some designs, but I don't like any of them.

Finally, I get an idea and call over the artist. He starts to sketch based on my description, and Clay watches.

"A mountain," I declare when it's done.

"For Denver," Clay reads, skeptical.

"No. Because they're the kind of strong the world can't break down. Not wind or rain or snow. They're weathered, but that only makes them more beautiful. Like you."

He takes me in, emotion flitting behind his eyes. "Sounds like a plan."

"Can you get it now?" I ask Clay.

He shakes his head. "We'd miss dinner."

"I'm okay with that."

Clay studies me a long moment, then cuts a look at the artist.

"Where'd you find her?" the artist asks Clay half an hour later.

"Wouldn't believe me if I told you."

Clay looks over at me under his dark lashes, and we exchange a grin.

Since the artist started to prep his tools, I've been peppering him with questions about his pigments and technique and what it's like to work on a human canvas.

Now, I'm sitting in a visitor's chair with my dress tugged down as far as possible thanks to the no underwear situation.

Clay is sitting astride another, elbows across the back as the mountain range is etched into his shoulder.

The buzzing of the needle blurs with the downtempo music from the speaker in the corner, a quiet symphonic background for what I'm witnessing.

It's beautiful.

The ink appears in soft strokes across Clay's smooth skin.

I thought the blood would bother me, but there's hardly any, and it's wiped away fast in a two-handed dance as elegant as any ballet.

Normally, the artist's calendar is booked for months, but apparently, he does all of Clay's tattoos, and he's the only client the artist would take on a walk-in basis. Especially on a Friday night.

"You decide what tattoo you want yet?" Clay asks, his face turned toward me.

He doesn't flinch or give any indication of the pain he's in. I wouldn't expect anything else from him.

"I thought it would be easy, but there are so many options." I glance around the studio, where art is mounted on every available surface. There are simple hearts and stars and banners along with photos of realistic faces, detailed mosaics and landscapes. "That's why you get one every year."

His eyes crinkle. "I get one every year because I'm in a different place. And it blurs together, but I don't wanna forget what got me here."

It humbles me even more that he let me help him pick one out. A tattoo to mark who he is, in this moment.

"You should've told me the assignment when I helped pick yours out," I chide him.

He rubs a hand over his jaw. "Nah. You aced it."

Clay orders dinner for the three of us, and on a break, we eat tacos wrapped in foil, as delicious as they are messy.

He also ordered me a bottle of wine delivered with chocolate-covered strawberries for dessert, so I'm riding a happy buzz.

When the artist stands up to stretch and use the bathroom, it's the two of us.

"Well?" Clay asks.

I inspect his back. There's a sun just appearing over the ridge.

"Is it rising or setting?" I ask.

"You tell me."

"Rising," I decide, and he grins.

∼

Once the tattoo is complete and covered, and we've said goodbye to the artist, we head back outside onto the sidewalk.

"I figured we'd see more stars," I say as we amble down the street.

"The city is too bright. Not like Red Rocks."

"No. But it's still beautiful."

There's a text from Mari saying she hopes I enjoy my mini trip, plus a picture of her and Harlan.

They look in love, and my heart squeezes. They have *everything*.

Is it so crazy to want that, too?

Not the perfect job or the man in a suit or the ring, but the happiness.

I tip my face up to stare at the sky.

He threads his fingers through mine. "I need to tell you something."

My heart accelerates. "Okay."

"I'm working on a trade to LA."

I stop walking and stare at him.

Guilt clouds his expression as I try to process what those words mean.

The most obvious one is he's not staying in Denver. He's switching sides, joining the same men who were his opponents tonight. Moving to this place of glitter and palm trees.

It hits me hard in the chest, though I can't point to exactly why. I'm not the one losing him, but it feels like a betrayal. "Does Harlan know?"

"No. And you can't tell him," Clay says firmly.

"Because you have a problem with him."

His lip curls. "Only problem I have is one he caused."

"Which is what, exactly?"

He shoves a hand through his hair but doesn't answer.

My head is still spinning about the rest of it as I pace the sidewalk. "I thought it was Harlan's job to sign off on that stuff."

"But he doesn't need to know I'm working on it until he gets an offer he can't refuse. Locker room rumors sink a team faster than anything, and I won't do that to the guys."

I get his reasoning, but hiding doesn't feel good. "I don't want to lie to my sister again."

"Aren't you already doing that by sneaking around with me?" Clay grabs my arms and spins me to face him.

I frown. "Why did you even tell me if you were going to put me in this position?"

He strokes my cheek with his thumb. "I guess because I'm used to keeping shit inside, and it feels good to tell someone. Plus, I don't like keeping it from you."

His words, or the vulnerability in them, make my frustration evaporate. What was going to be a hard decision is suddenly obvious.

"Then I won't say anything," I whisper.

Clay stills, his eyes widening with relief. "You mean it."

"Yeah." My lips curve.

He glances over his shoulder. "Come back to my room."

There's an urgency in his voice.

"That's not against the rules?"

He drags my mouth up to his, kissing me until I'm breathless. "I don't give a fuck."

24

CLAY

"All clear?" Nova whispers.

I look both ways. "For now."

We sneak down the hall to my hotel room. I fumble with my card before the light blinks, and we trip inside.

"Wow. This is what it's like to live the high life."

I can't help grinning. Some girls would care about amenities, want to hook up with me on the road in a five-star hotel.

She's not here for that.

Nova takes a tour, observing every inch of my one-night home while I observe her.

She's so beautiful. It's not only her pink hair and bright eyes and full lips. Not even her breasts that feel small and perfect in my hands or the addictive scent of her skin.

It's her openness and acceptance. How she's

game for anything and finds the sunshine on the darkest day.

Nova opens my fridge, eyes widening. "Holy. You could open a bar."

She takes one bottle after another and sets them out.

"I've never even heard of this," she says, inspecting a label.

"You want it?" I ask.

She turns it in her hands. "I had enough wine with dinner. But the bottle is pretty."

"Take it then. If you think it's pretty."

Nova smiles and sets it down. Then she lifts the lid of the silver pail nearby. "Huh. There's even ice in the bucket."

I shrug. "Turndown service."

She shakes her head as if it's the most ridiculous thing she's ever heard of. "So, you can't make your bed *or* unmake it without help? You're clearly overpaid."

Fuck, this girl is wild. I'm hanging on her every word.

The way she came apart under my hands in the limo was one thing. I was tempted to keep the car circling all night so I could pin her down on the seat and make her lose her mind until the only word she knew was my name.

But the fact that she promised to keep my secret means more.

People smile in my face all day long, but those who genuinely have my back are few and far between.

"Is your balcony connected to the others?" Nova opens the drapes and peers outside, oblivious to what's going on in my head.

"Yeah."

I come up behind her, and her body warms me.

"But here..." I place my hands on either side of her, my groin pressing against her back. "Glass feels thick enough to muffle the sounds."

Her head turns, her profile sheer temptation. "What sounds are those? You laughing at my jokes?"

"More like you moaning my name while I fuck you. Fast the first time, slow the second. The third, I'll let you choose," I murmur, claiming her lips from behind.

She tastes like wine. She's pliable, too, a little extra relaxed. I adjust her to face me, banging my leg into the window in the process.

"Your knee," she says when I wince, dropping the curtains back into place and pulling away.

"It's fine."

"Don't you usually take an ice bath?" Nova tries to slip out from under me.

Her happy buzz has vanished. I want it back.

I grab her wrist. "After."

"Clay—"

"Nova. I. Need. You," I say softly between kisses.

I press her back against the window until she melts again.

Tonight was good. I can't remember time spent with someone being so fulfilling. I liked being able to get her everything she wanted, but I also knew that she didn't care about any of it.

Nova fits in here. She'd fit in anywhere.

The rogue thought has my heart kicking. I always figured I had to go through this life alone, but who says I have to? She could stay as long as she wants. There'd be no karma to bite her. We'd have our thing until it ran its course…

Because she'd enjoy it.

Not because I'm not ready to let her go.

I spin and lift her, her dress riding up as her legs hook around my hips. I'm used to lifting hundreds of pounds, and she's nothing by comparison.

Nova grips my shoulders. Her body is sweet and soft, and I'm hard and hungry.

Back in the limo barely got me started. I want her all the ways there are. I want to turn her to liquid. To feel her melt around me, to absorb some of her fucking brightness.

I set her down long enough to yank down the zipper that holds up her dress and peel it off her. Beneath, she's naked.

"Christ." I take a moment to admire her.

She laughs, pressing a hand to her neck.

Her pale skin shines in the moonlight, the curve

of her breasts and swell of her hips making my throat dry with longing. I can't see the freckles that dust her shoulder, but I trace them from memory.

Her breasts are round and soft, and her pussy is fucking perfect.

"Too fucking pretty," I say as I sink to my knees.

Nova's thighs tremble as I kiss her soft skin. She leans into me.

"Are you ready again?" I ask.

"Are you kidding? It's like you have a magic touch."

She bends to reach for the buttons of my shirt, releasing them one by one until I can shrug out of it.

"I do. Especially when I'm with you."

I look up at her as I stroke her damp center with my fingers. Her lips part as I circle her clit with my thumb.

"Oh, God." She sways toward me, eyes drifting closed.

"I told you, sweetheart. My name is Clay."

I put my mouth to her and suck.

She moans.

Loud.

She's so damn sweet. Wet and wanting, arching against my face even as she bites her lip.

I'd give up oxygen if it meant staying right here forever.

"Yes, right there," she whispers. "You might have

a backup career. You know, if this basketball thing falls through."

I spread her wider, scraping my teeth lightly across her in retaliation.

Instead of squeaking, all she does is moan louder.

Well, fuck me. My sweet girl likes a little edge.

Her hands move to my head, her fingers tightening into my hair. I love it. It's her way of telling me what she needs.

Tonight, I'm going to take my time.

There's a knock on the other side of the windows. We can't see through the curtains, but Nova's eyes fly to mine.

"Ignore it," I rasp against her skin.

But she's torn between the interruption and me.

Fuck, that won't work.

I shove to standing.

It makes no sense for anyone to be on the balcony. Who'd be crazy enough to…

I tug back the edge of the curtains and look through the glass.

Rookie.

Ignoring him isn't an option thanks to Nova.

Murder isn't much better, though tossing him off the balcony right now holds some appeal.

I slide open the door enough to talk.

"What's up?" I ask in the most casual voice I can muster, the taste of Nova still on my tongue.

"I'm sorry about the game. I fucked up," he says.

My foot brushes something—her leather jacket. I bend to grab it and toss it out of sight.

"And you couldn't tell me another way?"

"I didn't want anyone to see." He hangs his head in shame. "Can I come in?"

I rub a hand over my face. "Hold on."

I go back to Nova. I lean over and murmur in her ear, "It's Rookie. I'll tell him we'll talk tomorrow."

She grabs the waist of my pants. "Clay, this is important. Talk to him now. Otherwise, he's going to lie awake all night feeling terrible."

"Maybe he should. And I can keep you awake all night feeling better than you've ever felt."

Nova reaches up to caress my neck. "As tempting as that sounds, I don't want to come between you and your team."

I want to tell her to forget him. Except...

She's so understanding.

It's part of why I like her so damn much.

I take her face in my hands and brush my lips over hers. "You're a good person."

She smiles. "I know. Now you go be one, too."

25

NOVA

I sneak a look at my phone before takeoff.

Grumpy Baller: Wish I could be there to hold your hand on the flight.

Nova: I'll grab on to Brooke :)

Last night, he took my idea of a date, doused it in gasoline, and set it on fire.

By the time I got back to my room, I stared at the ceiling and relived the entire night, starting with how he made me come in the limo and ending with the way he dropped to his knees and spread my thighs, licking me like it was the best part of his entire year.

At the time, I figured I was doing the right thing by taking a rain check on a night of sex with the hottest man I've ever met. But now, I'm mentally slapping myself.

"He's going to be a bear all week." Brooke drops into the seat next to me, tossing her braids over one shoulder.

I force myself to focus. "Jayden must take the loss hard."

"Not Jay. Miles."

I cock my head, curious. "Can you talk him down?"

"I could, but I won't. When he's in a shooting slump, candy works best. I'll send him gummy bears. How was your date last night?" Brooke leans in. "Sorry, your 'nap.'" She makes an up-and-down motion with one hand, and I laugh.

"I went with him to get a new tattoo."

"If a boy took me to get a tattoo, he wouldn't get another date."

"No, it was my idea. And it was incredible." I get dreamy thinking about it. "He even let me pick it out."

"Okay, that's kind of cute. So, where'd you make him put your initials?" Brooke lifts an eyebrow.

"Yeah, we're not that serious." I bite my lip. "But I like that we can confide in one another."

"Boy told you all his secrets, huh?"

I force a smile.

"A few."

I can't tell her about his plan to get traded,

because she's Jayden's sister, and I'm guessing Clay hasn't discussed this with his teammate. Usually I'm the one keeping secrets, and though I'm glad to have his, it's uncomfortable.

I check my email, but there's nothing.

"What's up?" Brooke asks.

"Just waiting on the head of my design firm saying I can come back to work."

"Do you even want to?"

"Of course I do. It wasn't a dream job, but I got to meet lots of people and sit in on cool design projects."

Brooke's face scrunches. "So, after the wedding, you'll go back to Boston. To the boring job, if they'll have you. And no hot guys."

"You make it sound awful," I say, tugging on a piece of my hair.

"We're young and hot and on a private plane. There's so much more living to do," Brooke insists.

I turn that over as we take off. Aside from gripping the armrest until my knuckles turn purple, I manage to survive.

Once we're up in the air, my stomach knots like it did on the flight to Denver. The one to LA wasn't so bad because we were talking about wedding stuff and guys and life. But now, Brooke's reading magazines on her phone.

I can entertain myself.

So, I go looking for my sketchpad in my bag. I've

finished my drawings of each of the starting five and am ready to start something new.

Maybe I'll draw Brooke.

I search the inside pockets and the outside ones. Nothing.

When was the last time I had it? I remember showing Clay but nothing after that.

I'll call the hotel when we land.

Short of launching myself off the plane in protest, there's nothing to be done in the meantime.

I pull up the internet on my phone and flip through images of Clay at the game. I deliberately ignore the ones where he's pissed and focus on him playing hard, dunking the ball, glaring at the other team's bench.

God, he's sexy.

I should've let him finish what he started last night.

With the wedding a week away, I don't even know when I'll get a chance to see him next.

I know his schedule is insanely demanding, but I want to spend time with him before I return to Boston or he gets his trade out of Denver, whichever comes first.

The idea of saying goodbye and never seeing him again makes my stomach wrench. But I'll deal with it when we get there.

"I think I'm going to donate a watch." Brooke's words bring my attention back.

"To what?"

"The Kodiak Foundation charity event is this weekend. You have to go."

"I'm pretty sure Mari will be in full wedding mode, and I'll back her up."

"All the team and families are invited. Which means Mari will be there, too."

And Clay. My heart leaps.

"Then I guess I'm in."

26

NOVA

"How was your LA trip with Brooke?" Mari asks as we get out of the car.

"Great. We did all the shopping. Okay, mostly she did," I amend.

"I hope the game wasn't too boring."

"Boring? Not at all. But not as exciting as tonight. You officially have a night off wedding planning," I declare as I link my arm through hers.

The charity auction takes place at a fancy hotel, with chandeliers and white fabric draping the walls. I expect to not recognize anyone, but there are actually a lot of familiar faces. Everyone I make eye contact with offers me a nod or a smile.

Since Brooke and I got back from LA, I've been focusing on Mari, including trying to find that song recording of my mom's. I could've sworn I had the file backed up. But after searching my phone and every cloud drive, I'm empty handed.

"Nova! It's so nice to see you again." Robin, dressed in a blue satin cocktail dress, embraces me when I arrive.

"You know one another?" Mari demands when Robin turns away.

I don't want to lie to my sister. "Yes," I say. "But Harlan swore me to secrecy."

Her eyes glint.

A tall, handsome guy pulls up next to Brooke before she can reply.

"This is my date," she says.

He introduces himself, flashing perfect teeth to go with his square jaw. "We went to school together. I'm in town for the week for work."

I scan the room. Harlan's on the other side, chatting up donors. I see Jayden in another circle of guys in suits.

It's a slice of what it must be like for the Kodiaks to be on the road and in a different city all the time.

Glamorous, sure.

But hard. Exhausting.

My gaze is drawn to Clay, deep in the heart of a crowd.

He texted to say that he'd had a good talk with Rookie. I'm so proud of him.

If only he could make peace with staying in Denver.

I did some searching online that corroborated the LA team is the top in the league. They have the biggest budget, the most glamorous profile, and they win.

I can understand why they would be appealing. But I wish he could be happy here, with what he has, and give the guys and the team a chance to see him as more than just the number of points he can put up in a night.

"Hey, Nova. You seen Brooke?" I'm waylaid by an irritated-looking Miles.

"She's over there." I point. "Everything okay?"

"Great." He rubs a hand over his smooth-shaven jaw. "Who's that guy?"

"Brooke's date. She knew him from school."

"She didn't go to school here."

I shrug. "I guess he wanted to see her."

Miles looks desperate. "That why she said she couldn't dog-sit for me earlier today?" He grunts something I can't hear before stalking off.

I bite the inside of my cheek. Apparently, I'm not the only one with guy drama.

The beautiful tables are laid out with auction merchandise that will be sold in a few minutes. Maybe I'll buy myself a treat.

"Do I need an Apple Watch?" an older man in a suit with graying hair asks me.

It takes a second for me to recognize him as the

Kodiaks' coach. It's the first time I've seen him up close.

"I'm not the person to ask." I hold up my bare wrist. "But I hear it tracks all sorts of data and metrics."

"Well, I don't want to put the assistant coaches out of work." His eyes crinkle, and I laugh.

"I'm Nova, Harlan's future sister-in-law."

"Call me Bill. And I know who you are," he says, eyes sparkling. "I've seen you drawing up in the box."

My gaze flies to Clay, but Coach continues down the row of items for auction.

"You seem to be fitting in well."

"I'm only here until the wedding. It feels strange to get to know people only to leave them again."

"Describes nearly every job in the NBA," he says dryly.

That never occurred to me. "But surely people can build a career in a city if they want to. Harlan's here to stay—he has a house and an office and five cars."

"Five, huh?"

Coach laughs, and I blush. Maybe that wasn't public knowledge.

"From the scouts to the GMs to the players, we drag our asses across the country and around the world for the chance to be a part of this sport we love. The moment you think you have control, you realize you're at the whim of something bigger."

I think about Clay's stress over his injuries, his desire to play where he can make a name for himself. Or build on the one he has.

Everyone on the team wants the same things, but they need to realize it.

I scan the ballroom and send off a text.

Nova: I need your help.

It's not a minute later when I feel him come up behind me.

"Hello there."

"Hi."

I turn and smile up into Clay's handsome face. In a suit, he looks incredible.

"Coach and I were just talking…"

I turn and gesture to the man behind me, and Clay realizes he's been caught out.

"He was wondering about this Apple Watch. I figured since you're so into technology, with your electric car and everything, you could advise him."

Clay's eyes narrow. *I'm on to you.*

I shrug, innocent. *What?*

But the two men start to talk, and satisfaction rises up in me. I've given him the perfect opportunity to mend fences. Maybe even to talk about his future here.

I continue down toward the auction table, proud of my job well done.

My attention locks onto a display of frames.

The contents are intimately familiar, and my heart starts to thud.

"Wait, what are...?"

My drawings.

Five of them.

One for each of the starters, including Clay.

"They're stunning," a woman next to me says. "A good idea to get them signed by the players."

Because, I realize, they are signed by the players.

～

After dinner and the auction, I'm still in shock.

Someone put my images up for auction. And people bought the pieces, one after another.

More than seventy thousand dollars for charity.

Until the one of Clay was scheduled to come up and the auctioneer conferred with a colleague before coming back to the mic. "I've been informed this piece was acquired by a private collector for an unnamed amount."

The crowd groaned.

Robin finds me after it's over. "Nova, that was a very generous contribution."

"How did I not know you were doing this?" Mari demands. "Is this what you've been doing sneaking around and spending all that time around the team?"

"It's wonderful." Harlan nods in appreciation.

"But... how did you get them signed?" Mari asks.

"I helped." Brooke loops an arm around my waist, a coy smile on her face.

Then who did this?

I can't ask, not here.

She turns back to her date, and I sneak outside to the pool for a breath of fresh air. The patio area is empty at night, the bright-blue lights of the pool shimmering.

I suck in oxygen, grateful for a moment alone to process.

I've never dared to put myself out there. Since art school, I haven't had an exhibition. This was unplanned. The emotions rushing up, hope and gratitude and excitement, are overwhelming.

"You are sneaky, trying to get me and Coach on good terms again."

The familiar voice and footsteps at my back make me turn.

Clay hovers in the doorway a dozen feet away.

The tips of his tattoos creep out of his collar. He's like an animal playing at being tame.

"It's a benefit for you and for the team. You mad?"

He takes leisurely steps across the pool area until he stops next to me, hands in the pockets of his tux.

"I'll get over it."

His smile feels like a secret between us. "And

what about you? You're the woman of the hour in there."

I press my hands to my chest. "Those sketches were some of the first I've done in ages. Now they belong to people I've never met. Because of you."

No one else knew about my drawings or would have had the motive.

"You're pissed." He doesn't try to deny it.

"Yes. No."

I love my art. I'd be flattered and excited if anyone showed an interest in my drawings.

"It's incredible people would pay that much for signatures," I say at last.

"They'd pay that much for your art," he corrects. "You see people in a way that's better than how they see themselves. I wish you could see yourself like I see you."

"How is that?"

In the water, our silhouettes are reflected from the lights behind us, his dark eyes holding mine prisoner in our shared reflection.

"When I see your drawings, I see you. You're brave and kind and so fucking beautiful it hurts to look at you."

My heart beats in my ears. "No one's ever done anything like this for me."

"Stolen your possessions and auctioned them off?"

"Exactly. Thank you." I stare out at the lights

shining over the pool, feeling like I'm seen and like I belong. In the last place I expected, I feel like I belong. "Even Harlan looked happy," I go on. "He's good for Mari. I can't imagine a better guy to have in the family, even if you and he don't see eye to eye."

His smile fades. "You remember the girl back in college that cheated on me and the entire team lied about it? Harlan was the one who told them to keep it quiet."

My heart wrenches at the bitterness in his voice. "I don't believe—"

"It's true. I caught them two weeks before Finals. She admitted it had been going on and who had helped cover it up. It was Harlan's idea not to tell me so it wouldn't mess with my game. He knew the entire semester but decided that winning mattered more than the truth."

My chest tightens. "I'm sorry. That must have been hell."

"For a while. Then it didn't." He doesn't explain more. "I decided she was dead to me and so was management. I played out of my mind so that I never had to rely on suits or anyone else ever again."

"And it worked," I murmur.

He became an all-star. Revered. Untouchable.

"Maybe Harlan made a mistake. Maybe he's changed."

"I don't care if he has. I'm not giving him another chance to burn me like that."

I understand a little more why he's closed off the way he is, why trusting people in general and Harlan in particular feels dangerous.

I can't help asking, "Was she the last woman you loved?"

Clay shifts on his feet. "Could be it wasn't even love. I'm not sure I'm made for that."

My heart aches for him, for the fact that he's missing out on the beauty that can happen when you let another person in.

Not like I'm the poster child for choosing romantic partners, but I want to believe in that kind of love.

A sound outside reminds me where we are. That there are people who'll notice soon that we're gone, if they haven't already.

"Harlan's marrying my sister in two more days," I say quietly. "I get that you have history, but they're happy. I won't let anything get in the way of that."

"No inviting a herd of LA fans to crash the wedding. Got it."

My lips twitch. "Now if only I could find this song of our mom's. I thought I could fit it into the music during the ceremony to surprise her. It would be like Mom and Dad were there."

His hand brushes mine, and he laces our fingers together. "You have a good heart, Pink. You'll figure it out."

We stand like that for a minute or five. I don't want to move, just be here with him.

"So, someone bought you," I comment. "I wonder how much they paid."

He grins. "Not enough."

27

CLAY

"That's a foul," I say evenly.

Nine other players on the court pull up and look toward me.

"What? No way." Rookie's standing a few strides away from where he ripped the ball from my hands a second ago.

"It's a foul." I take it back and demonstrate.

"You do that all the time," he protests. "They don't call you on it."

"That's because I'm me. For the next year or two, you're you."

He curses colorfully.

I grab his shoulder and pull him in.

"Hey. You survive that time, you get the benefit of the doubt. Until then, you go the fuck to work and show them why you deserve it. Now go again."

Rookie sighs but sets up to guard me one more time.

I feel Jay's eyes on me through the entire play, until the assistant overseeing our drill calls a break.

"What?" I ask my friend.

"You're being nicer to Rookie since the charity auction. Since LA, in fact."

I lift a shoulder. "He's here if I like him or not. Maybe he'll get my laundry done right."

"You mean you like him," Jay laughs.

For the past week, life has been extra busy.

Harlan's wedding is this weekend. We're hurtling toward the season.

We played our final two preseason road games, winning them both.

My downtime's been spent with the entire team packed into Bear Force One.

I've barely seen Nova.

There's nothing like the high of victory. It's what I live for.

But I miss her face. Miss the sound of her voice.

We text every day, talk when we can.

I asked for a picture, and she sent me one of her in the jersey I gave her, annotated on the screen with text that read "LEFT" and an arrow helpfully pointing to one of her tits.

Joke's on her because I still got off to that picture lying in a hotel bed in Phoenix.

We haven't had a minute in private, but every

time I close my eyes on a plane or when I fall into bed, she's there.

I hadn't realized I could be this obsessed about anything but basketball.

Even now, as I'm standing here in a gym filled with the guys I train with and professionals of every kind, all I can think of is the last time I saw her.

She grounds me. As if even in my darkest moments, I might be someone worth saving. A man whose worth goes deeper than the court.

"How long before we're done with this?" I ask Jay.

He glances at his watch. "An hour."

"What's on your mind?" Jay asks me.

I'm a grown man. Not a teenager with a crush. I don't do this shit.

"There's this woman."

"You mean Nova."

"I mean Nova."

He grins at me like the cat that ate the canary.

"What?" I say, affronted. "It's not like I'm here every night thinking about her."

"No, but you don't have her here with you, so you think about her."

"Fuck you."

He laughs. "If I had a girl like Nova, I wouldn't let her out of my sight."

"No shit."

"You don't do relationships," he says.

"I know."

"But?"

I shrug. "I don't know. Everything's different with her."

I want to show her.

After the wedding, once she has a second to think about herself and not her sister.

I head to the bleachers and grab my phone from my bag to see if she's texted.

There's a voicemail from my agent.

"Good news. LA's putting something together. Guess your performance instilled confidence you're still the guy to have for their title run. But word is, Harlan refused to take the call."

Anger burns through me.

Tonight is the rehearsal dinner. The entire starting lineup was invited, but it was a formality. I was planning to go so I could stare at Nova from across the room, maybe drag her into the coat check at the end of the night.

But my feelings for her are overrun by my frustration with Harlan.

The assistant coaches run the team through more drills.

I grab the ball and go in for a drive, going hard at the defense. They stand their ground, and I twist, going down hard.

My knee screams.

I grunt, swallowing the sharp pain as one of the trainers motions me over.

"That looked rough," he says.

"It's fine. I'll walk it off."

The joint twinges as if silently arguing with me.

Coach crosses to us. "You came down on it hard."

I take a deep breath.

If I'm hurt, LA won't want me again. No one will.

I'll be collecting a paycheck and riding the bench for some team, forced to watch the other guys fight night after night at the only thing I've ever been good at.

The trainer pulls up something on his phone. "We can get you in for treatment tonight."

"Tonight's the rehearsal dinner," Jay reminds me.

I exhale hard. "I'll come later. This matters more."

28

NOVA

The rehearsal dinner is supposed to be casual, but it's still two dozen of Harlan and Mari's friends and extended family.

When we arrive at dinner, Jay, Miles, and Atlas are there, but there's no sign of Clay.

"He's coming," I say under my breath. "He's just running late."

Chloe and I have already talked about positions, so I know I'm sitting in the middle of the table with Jay to my left. Atlas is next to him, along with Miles.

When I sit, Mari takes a seat next to Harlan.

I send off a text to ask Clay where he is. I'm doing my best not to let my worry show, but I can't help it.

"I have a special present for my new wife," Harlan announces from the head of the table before nodding to Robin. "Mari, in honor of our marriage, I've created a new scholarship named after your family and to be administered by the Kodiaks foundation. It will help fund education for young women."

My sister's eyes fill. "Oh, Harlan. I'm so touched."

Everyone cheers and toasts, but I'm distracted until Harlan adds, "Special thank you to Nova for helping make this happen."

Mari looks between us in disbelief.

I wish Clay were here to see this because I'm so proud and because I want him to see that Harlan is the kind of man who cares about people. No matter what went down in college, he's not "basketball at all costs."

For a moment, I imagine him standing in Harlan's place, giving me a surprise gift that's thoughtful and generous.

I imagine I'm so in love my insecurities run wild, only to be comforted the moment I look in his eyes. I picture him putting me first the way Harlan does with Mari.

The idea lingers as we eat prime rib and rich fluffy potatoes, drink champagne, and talk in excited voices about tomorrow.

"Earth to Nova." Brooke's voice breaks my reverie.

I blink, coming out of my head. "What?"

She's looking at me oddly. "Where's Clay?"

I shrug. "I don't know."

Jay leans in. "Something came up after practice."

He doesn't say more, and I try not to worry about what that might mean.

I'm already a few glasses in when the text comes through.

Grumpy Baller: I'm not going to make it tonight.

Nova: What happened? Everything okay?

Grumpy Baller: Yeah. Just basketball stuff.

I'm waiting for the rest of the explanation, but it never comes.

He's just going to let it go like I don't deserve an explanation?

Or he's working on that trade.

I excuse myself to run to the bathroom. On my way, I set my empty champagne flute on the bar.

I know Clay isn't Harlan's biggest fan, but I'm the one who feels let down. As if he's not here because he doesn't care enough about me.

I'm pulling open the bathroom door when I hear my name.

I turn to see Jay.

"Sorry about Clay."

My stomach sinks, and I can't help but feel disappointed.

"Yeah. Me, too," I say.

Jay shifts on his feet. "He's been through some shit."

"Such as?" I ask.

"I don't know if it's my place to say anything," he finally replies.

Maybe I can't trust Clay. He hasn't told Jayden about his mission to get traded, and he obviously hasn't told me everything about his past.

I give myself a few minutes to be sad before I leave the bathroom and continue to the private party room.

When I return, I can hear my family laughing and talking.

Atlas, Miles, and Chloe have joined them, and it feels like a happy party.

I don't belong in the celebration, and I don't belong with them.

Brooke teases me, and Miles sneaks looks at her. Harlan beams at Mari with pride. I ignore the spot that's conspicuously empty.

When dessert is served, it's a rich chocolate mousse.

I force myself to stop looking toward the door.

He's always going to let me down, and it's better to know now.

I won't make another mistake with him.

I won't let it be like everything else in my life.

29

NOVA

The wedding day is cold and clear.

I get out of the shower to find a voicemail from Clay.

My heart pounds as I hit Play.

"Pink, listen, about last night... I was feeling like shit after practice, and it threw me. But that's no excuse. I fucked up. Jay told me about the scholarship. I know how important that was to you, and I wish I'd been there to see your sister's face. And to tell you how damn proud I am of you." His voice drops. "I'm gonna make it up to you. Can't tell you how because it's a surprise. But I can't wait to see you in that dress."

My chest expands when I hang up.

He sounds so earnest and contrite.

Clay isn't Brad. He's not careless with my

feelings, and I'm not some pawn in a secret game to him.

His life is complicated, and he invited me in rather than holding me at a distance.

But is it enough? I can't throw my heart recklessly after him. He has trust issues, and I'm finally realizing what it means to take care of myself.

I start to tuck my phone away but notice a red notification with the number one hovering over my email.

I click it open.

Nova,

We've cleared you of wrongdoing and regret any inconvenience this may have caused. We'd like you to resume your job at the earliest opportunity.

Sincerely,

Mr. Dalton

It's what I've wanted for the past month.
Exoneration.
A way forward.
But with it, there's a new tension in my body.

Getting what I've been desperate for all along doesn't feel as good as I expected.

I vow to push the news, and my complicated reaction, out of my mind for the rest of the day.

This is about my sister, I remind myself as I bound down the stairs to grab coffee for Mari and myself.

"What are you doing down here?!" Brooke grabs my shoulders ninety minutes later at the venue.

"Fixing flowers." My face screws up as I adjust the swag on the end of the rows of chairs.

"You need to get dressed." She's already in her bridesmaid's dress, the soft pink making her golden skin glow. I'm still wrapped in a robe, but guests won't be arriving for another hour at least. "Hey!" she calls to a tall, broad figure in a dress shirt crossing the hall. "Come tell Nova these flowers are perfect."

Miles is wearing a dark suit with a baby-blue shirt that sets off his blue eyes. His gaze locks on Brooke, and he does a double take. "Ladies." He adjusts his suit as he crosses to us. "You look..."

Brooke cocks her head.

"Elegant."

My friend laughs. "Thanks."

I glance down at my robe and flip-flops.

"How long have you been my brother's best friend?"

"Forever."

"Which means you have to do what I say."

"That's not what it—"

"Like take care of these flowers while Nova gets ready."

Brooke blinks up at him, her eyes wide with intention.

He's crumbling.

All six-five of Miles seems to bend. "Anything for you."

Brooke beams at me, triumphant. "We'll take care of this."

∼

"What's wrong?" I ask when I head up the stairs to find a worried-looking Chloe emerging from the dressing room.

"She doesn't want to get ready."

"Mari?" I knock on the door. "It's time to go."

I tug at the neckline of the dress I just put on.

She doesn't answer, and I push the door open to find my sister wrapped in her robe, clutching her bridal gown and wearing one high heel while squinting at the other held close to her face.

"Are you almost ready?" I ask.

"My dress doesn't fit," she says. "And my shoe is broken. And the wedding is in two hours," she says, "and I can't walk down the aisle with one shoe. People will laugh, and my life will be over."

She's having a meltdown.

For a second, I'm at a loss. I've never seen my big sister looking so out of it.

"I'm sure the dress fits." We just tried it three days ago.

I help her into it and zip her up.

The dress is tight, which is exactly how it's made to be.

"There. You look perfect."

"Except for my shoes."

One of them is broken. There's a rip in the cream satin covering the heel.

"These were designer," Mari groans. "They cost more than my first car."

I step out of mine and slide them over.

"What will you wear?"

"I can go barefoot." I grin.

"No, you won't."

"Fine, I'll fix yours."

"You can't just glue them."

I pull at the right side of the heel, trying to tuck the satin edge in. When I release it, the fabric sags again, flopping open like a gaping wound.

"Broken. I told you," Mari insists.

"I can fix it." I lean over the shoe.

Her eyes fill with tears. "You can't fix it, Nova. It's too late."

I set the heel down and take her hand. "I'm sorry I couldn't find that recording of Mom singing. I know how special it was to you and how much it would have meant to include it. I'm sorry I've let you down in the past. I'm sorry if I didn't notice when you were struggling. But we're all doing our best, Mar. What looks easy from the outside isn't always"—I think of Clay—"and even when things aren't perfect..." I take my sister's face in my hands, careful not to smudge her makeup. "They can be really good."

My sister blinks as if seeing me for the first time.

"Now come on," I say with a smile. "Let's get you to your wedding."

We head down the stairs, and my attention catches on the flowers pinned to the railing.

The wire is covered in white satin.

I unwind a strip, and a flower comes off with it. Mari gasps. "What are you doing?"

I hold out a hand for the shoe, and she passes it to me, still shocked.

I take the shoe and use the strip of decorated wire to wrap around the fabric, covering the tear.

"There."

"It's not even." She hesitates. "Do the other one, too?"

∽

It's not until all the girls are finally ready to walk down the aisle that I miss Mom and Dad.

Now I'm sitting at the end of the aisle, feeling a

pang of regret that they weren't here to watch Mari walk down the aisle, too.

I can't think about that now, with the music swelling and my sister's face peeking out from the doorway.

The music starts, and the procession begins.

On my walk down the aisle, I don't see the guys, but when I turn to face the rows of guests, it's impossible to miss the tall, handsome men in the back.

Mari appears at the end of the aisle. Her hair is half twisted up and half loose, the mermaid dress sexy and modern and so very Mari. I'm thrilled to see her so happy.

Pictures snap.

Mari smiles, her eyes only on Harlan, and starts down the aisle, a riot of pink flowers erupting from her hands, shades matching her lipstick and flushed cheeks.

She looks every bit the bride, even in a broken shoe, and I don't notice the flower until she's almost at the front.

I rub the back of my neck to ease the tension. It's not that big a difference.

But it is.

A small sign of her meltdown. It's the tiniest crack in perfection.

It's a relief somehow.

She reaches Harlan, who looks every bit as stunned as her.

Tingling draws my attention to the crowd, and I catch Clay watching me.

His gaze warms me.

He's gorgeous in a dark suit, his tattoos invisible except for that trail inching up his neck. I don't know when he got here, but I'm glad he did. I offer a tiny smile, and he returns it.

The officiant starts the wedding, and I focus on that. Not the dreams that seeing Clay in a church has suddenly sent spiraling through my mind.

When they exchange vows, I allow myself a moment to daydream.

"Nova, you're my forever.

I'll put you first.

Love you and cherish you.

I'll be here when you're at your best and worst."

I want to believe there's a chance for Clay and me. Not some wild adventure, but a chance for a real relationship and future.

Brooke slips me a tissue, and that's when I realize my eyes are damp.

The vows conclude, and Harlan and Mari kiss to deafening cheers. They sign the register with Chloe and Harlan's best man, and we cluster around for pictures at the altar.

Once everything is signed, the happy couple rises and prepares for the recessional. Mari's eyes meet mine, and I can tell she's thrilled, but there's a fleeting sadness.

The song Mom used to sing isn't playing during this special moment.

I cross to Mari and hug her, and she hugs me back before pulling away to take Harlan's arm.

Before they can descend the steps from the altar, a choir stands at the back and starts to sing.

My sister freezes as the words to "Home" stream out in a dozen voices.

Mari gasps, pressing her arm holding her bouquet to her face.

I swallow hard. Clay meets my eyes.

By the second verse, Mari and Harlan descend the steps. She's smiling and crying, her lips trembling as she leans on her new husband.

Clay gives me that nod.

That "secret smile" nod.

That "I did the only thing in the world that could have made this day better" nod.

My heart starts up, and I don't know how long it had been stopped for.

∽

The photographer comes and sweeps us off immediately after the ceremony. I manage to sneak out my phone while we're on our way to where we'll shoot pictures.

Grumpy Baller: You look beautiful.

The message comes through in between poses.

Nova: You don't look so bad yourself. If you're lucky, I'll save you a dance.

In the gardens, we pose in small and large groups with the happy couple. After what feels like hundreds of pictures, my phone goes off again.

Grumpy Baller: I'm taking all of them.

~

By the time we get back from photos, the reception is bursting with guests. Every surface is covered in flowers with soft lights strung up in the vaulted ceiling of the hallway. The wedding party and the newlyweds are announced and seated at the head table.

The MC, Harlan's best man, runs through opening comments plus a few jokes about him that have everyone cracking up before he introduces Chloe.

She rises and goes to the front. With a smile as genuine as it is easy, she talks about how they met and bonded. We're all drawn in. Not a person in the crowd isn't captivated, including the players. Jay's leaning in, elbows on the table and brows pulled together as if you couldn't pry him away for anything.

"And I hope we'll have so many adventures and stories. For someone who already has those, I want to turn it over to Mari's sister, Nova."

My throat swells.

I rise from my seat and head to the podium.

"Sorry to put you on the spot," she whispers. "Mari thought you wouldn't mind."

I stare out at the crowd and at my sister. Mari's smiling my way, and my chest expands.

"I honestly wasn't expecting to do this. It's like winning an Oscar and not having planned your speech."

There are a few chuckles.

Clay catches my eye and nods.

"Siblings are people who have to love us no matter what. There were a few times over the years I would've walked away if we weren't blood." A few more chuckles sound through the audience. "But Mari never did. I always wanted to be like my big sister, and now I see I can't be like her. But I can be there for her. I can only hope that one day we're all as lucky as you both are."

Mari's eyes are damp as she reaches for Harlan's hand.

I raise my glass. "To love that finds us when we need it, not when we're looking. May your hearts always surprise you in the best ways."

Everyone repeats and clinks their glasses.

I take a sip, the bubbles dancing down my throat. I feel Clay's eyes on me the entire time.

"That was really good," Brooke says, hooking an arm around me when Harlan and Mari go for their first dance.

We watch them twirl slowly on the floor.

"You going to do that someday?" I ask.

"Get married? Never."

I laugh. "What if you find the right person?"

"No such guy. It's better to live your life on your own terms."

I'm in line for the powder room when I read the email again.

"Thank you for everything." My attention snaps up and I see Harlan emerge.

"My pleasure. It's been a beautiful day."

His brows draw together as he takes in my expression. "Everything okay?"

I nod and tell him about the email from my boss.

"That's good," he prompts.

"Yes. It is."

With a perplexed smile, Harlan excuses himself.

It is good. It's a chance to move forward without the shadow of my ex looming over me.

It's the proof that I can handle my own life, even if my life isn't as thrilling as my sister's or a professional athlete's.

After checking my makeup in the mirror, I head back out.

There're several couples and groups already dancing, and I linger at the edge of the floor watching.

Someone taps my shoulder. I turn to find Clay staring down at me, his smoldering intensity on full display.

"Dance with me."

I take his hand, and he leads me to the floor.

There are eyes on us. I feel them.

"I know you're not Harlan's biggest fan, or Mari's," I say. "So, thank you. For what you did for my sister."

"I didn't do it for her. I did it for you."

I stare up at him, his hands warm on mine.

At the front of the room, words were easy.

Now, there's nothing to say to capture what I'm feeling. What I want. What I hope.

"First game of the season is Tuesday," Miles interrupts from where he's dancing with his date. "Don't screw up your knee."

"I can still beat you on one leg."

Miles laughs, and we make another few turns to the music.

Across the room, Mari and Harlan are engrossed in talking to their guests. I watch them disappear out to the garden with some friends, each with a glass of wine in hand.

I don't know what the future holds. I thought all I wanted was to be on stable ground, to have people see me as an adult who has her life together. But right now, I'm enjoying being exactly where I am.

Now, there's a streak of independence, of adventure, I didn't bank on. It has something to do with the man holding me in the middle of the dance floor.

"The day I met you, I was dreading coming back for the season. I was in a dark mood, and this pixie on the plane who had no idea who I was stole my seat. The way you argued, lost, then decided we should be friends, I thought you were crazy," Clay murmurs into my hair. "But there was something underneath the pink hair and the tequila shots. You cared about people, and it drew me to you from the start."

I sigh, content. "I thought you were some asshole gym owner," I admit, and he grins. "You were too cool for me until you agreed to switch seats. You ripped my *Sports Illustrated* magazine like a psycho—"

"They had a feature on me. I didn't want to ruin what we had going on."

My lips part, and it takes a moment for me to continue. "You followed me into the bathroom because you were worried. You worried about a stranger, and it was the sweetest thing anyone's ever done for me."

We turn in circles, Clay holding me close.

"And here I thought it was my tattoos that got you through."

I bite my cheek. "Guys don't normally strip for me in bathrooms. It might have helped a little."

Beneath the humor, I see the truth.

He's been there all along, the person who knows me, who backs me up no matter the cost. The man who made me believe life doesn't have to go in one direction.

"What are you thinking?" he murmurs, his fingertips brushing my neck, sending tingles from my neck straight down my body.

"I'm thinking I really like that you're here."

His eyes hold mine, and what passes between us is more than I ever dared to hope for.

"We never finished our game from the plane," he says.

I flash back to Two Truths and a Lie. "Only because you didn't follow the rules and refused to take a turn."

His thumbs stroke down my bare arms. "Fine, here goes." He clears his throat. "One, I don't hate Denver as much as I used to."

My lips twitch.

"Two, my knee is less fucked than I thought."

He trails off, and I pull back enough to look up at him.

"And?"

Clay looks past me. "Three...I'm falling for a girl.

I never expected it to happen. I never looked for her. But she found me anyway. And I'm really fucking glad she did."

My chest tightens.

"Please don't joke about that," I whisper.

"You think I am?"

"You're Clayton Wade. You barely let anyone in. You don't fall."

He pulls me closer. "You said yourself—people change."

My heart thuds.

I want the physical connection, but I want more than that, too.

I want him to see all of me, even the things I'm trying not to look at.

But this is the first time he's said anything hinting at a future.

What would that even mean? He's about to embark on his season, a demanding rush of grueling games and media appearances, not to mention his secret ambition to land himself in a job halfway across the country.

"I spent the last month putting myself back together," I start. "Spending time with you helped, I won't pretend it didn't. But I don't want to just be someone you pick up and put down when it's convenient."

"I know. And I'm not that guy," Clay says, his

voice low and urgent. "Let me take you home and prove it to you."

My heart hammers against my ribs. "After Harlan and Mari leave."

He brushes his lips along my throat, making me shiver.

"After."

30

CLAY

"The fuck are you doing?" I ask Miles as I join him in the dark yard.

Most of the guests are inside, dancing and drinking and celebrating. The cold evening makes the hairs lift on my arms even through my shirt and suit jacket.

"Waffles needed to use the little Frenchies' room." I follow his line of sight to see the dog in question, wearing a bowtie and pawing the lawn with enthusiasm.

"You're freezing your balls off out here," Jay grunts as he comes out, Coach on his heels.

"It's exposure therapy. Good for the muscles," Miles tosses back.

I glance toward the window. Inside, Brooke's dancing with Nova and Chloe.

Tonight has been something else.

Nova looks gorgeous in that dress. I wanted to drag her off with me.

To touch every inch of her.

But it's more than that.

So much fucking more.

I meant it when I said I was falling for her. That part wasn't a lie, even if it would be easier if it were.

She's the person who holds me down when I'm drifting, who lifts me up when I'm heavy.

She's the best thing in my life.

In a few hours, I'll show her.

"Wade." Harlan's voice makes me turn. "A word."

He cocks his head, and the other guys head inside with murmured words of support.

Coach is the last one in, patting Harlan on the shoulder.

"I suppose this is where I say congratulations," I say.

A waiter drifts past, offering champagne, and I wave him off.

"You almost seem like a romantic. If I didn't know better, I would've guessed you were too busy decorating this place and visiting with your family to take LA's calls." I glance at his breast pocket, the outline of the phone there.

His eyes crinkle. "I don't want to trade you, Clay. I believe in you and what you can do, even if I'm the last person you'd want as a cheerleader."

"I'd say less cheerleader, more puppet master."

My eyes narrow as I think of his manipulations.

"I know you didn't appreciate my efforts to intervene in college. But I did it to protect your future. You were having an MVP season. I didn't want to see anyone get in the way of that."

The music blurs together in the background.

I look back to the window again. This time Nova's in there with her sister, and they're hugging.

"I saw you and Nova dancing." Harlan changes the subject, and my shoulders tighten under my jacket. "For weeks, I was impressed she'd taken an interest in the sport. Her drawings were remarkable. But it wasn't basketball that caught her eye."

I don't answer.

"I'm sure you know that she got offered her job back in Boston." My head snaps up, and he can see immediately this is news to me. "She's had a hell of a time, and it's the fresh start she wanted. I hope you'll let her have it."

I stop the waiter on his return trip to the house and snatch a glass of champagne. "I might have to listen to you when we're in the stadium, but I don't take life advice from you anymore."

"It's not advice—it's the truth. She's never had the chance to stand on her own feet. Her piece-of-shit ex is out of the picture, and she can figure out who she wants to be. She won't do that next to you."

The words bury themselves deep in my chest, burrowing like shards of glass.

"What are you talking about?"

"To be truly great, you have to be relentless. To block everything else out. The only family is the other four guys on the court. You want glory, there's a price."

I toss the champagne back in one gulp.

Inside, Nova laughs, and seeing a smile on her face dissolves the pain for an instant.

She's beautiful.

She looks around as if searching for someone.

Me.

It's me she's looking for.

I can give her everything.

I'll buy her an entire studio where she can paint, fly her anywhere in the world to find the perfect tattoo, hold her hand the entire way there.

"Priorities change." I turn back to Harlan, setting my glass on a table.

"So, basketball doesn't come first." It's a question framed as a statement.

"She matters," I say instead.

It's not an answer. We both know it.

"I'm glad to hear that because it makes what I have to say next easier." Harlan studies me hard. "Feelings have a way of changing all our priorities, mine included. I hoped you'd become a legend here, that you'd give me the time to persuade you. But you don't want that. You want to play for LA. Yes, I know about your little side project," he goes on at my expression. "Ordinarily we'd discuss it like equals, but I can see you're beyond reasoning. So," he takes a breath, "if you give up Nova, I'll trade you to LA. You'll be an NBA champion. You'll have greatness, and she'll have the chance to live her own life."

My knee throbs.

There's a twisting in my chest.

No. The word is on the tip of my tongue.

LA is exactly what I wanted. But it doesn't feel like enough.

I want to toss his offer back at him.

I can give her everything.

Except not the everything she wants.

I never thought I'd see things Harlan's way, but in this moment, I get it.

He can't give me what I need here.

I can't give Nova what she needs.

What if he's wrong? A voice whispers.

"You think I don't remember what happened in college?" he prompts. "The fallout after, the shit you don't talk about? You want to put that on her?"

My palms start to sweat.

I've been honest with her, more open than I've been with anyone in a long time.

Still...

There are secrets buried so deep we don't ever talk about them.

Moments so dark they block out the light.

"Give her space to decide her future without the pressure of yours," Harlan urges.

She wants her sister, forgiveness, a chance to stand on her own feet.

The throbbing gets worse. In my knee, in my chest.

Harlan holds out his hand.

31

NOVA

"You're pink," Mari says, pressing a finger into the pinned-up curls on my head.

"You're drunk."

"I'm not," she protests, throwing her arms around me. "I'm only tipsy," she whispers.

"Got it," I laugh.

"This is the best night of my life."

"You're the most beautiful bride, Mar."

She beams. "Thank you. I'm going to say goodbye to the rest of the wedding party, then Harlan and I are leaving for our honeymoon."

She whooshes off to Chloe, who gestures and mouths to me, "Sparkler send off in ten?"

I nod, satisfaction and love welling up inside me.

I'm bursting with them.

My future is far from settled, but tonight has been amazing.

I'm tipsy on wine and swaying to the band as they play old favorite songs. I scan the crowd of well-dressed, beautiful, and generally tall people looking for one in particular.

"Nova."

The familiar voice has me turning.

"Harlan." I throw my arms around him, significantly more buzzed than the last time I bumped into him, and he's surprised a second before he hugs me back. "You're a married man. Ready to start the season with new commitments."

"And I couldn't be happier."

He looks as if he means it.

"When you were growing up, did you ever think you'd be here?" I ask him.

"I can honestly say it never occurred to me."

"Me either. This entire month has been a trip," I say. "I'm glad we're family. That I get to know you."

His eyes cloud. "So am I. I hope you know you're always welcome here, even after you go back to Boston."

I twist my hands together, anticipation bubbling up. "I haven't decided if I will."

"Oh?"

"I might try something new. I don't have to have my entire life figured out yet, right?"

I flush and scan the crowd. Still no sign of Clay.

"You certainly don't." Harlan sounds thoughtful.

I reach for my phone to see if there are any texts.

Nothing.

"Nova..."

"Sorry." I tuck the phone away. "I just—"

I look at the slip of paper in Harlan's hand. "What is that?"

Instead of a guestbook, Harlan and Mari had people write on sheets of paper and slip them into a box with their hopes or advice for the couple.

"Is that my name?" I ask, spotting the handwriting on the half-folded sheet.

Harlan's face tightens. In my happy, buzzed state, I reach for it without waiting for a response.

The moment I feel the paper against my fingers, I have the sudden impulse to give it back.

"It's time to do the sparklers!" Brooke shouts, descending from nowhere with a handful of the things.

She shoves them into my free hand, and I nod quickly. "I'll be right there!"

"Hurry up. Miles almost burned his hands off the last time he tried to do this. We need as much supervision as possible."

"Thank you for everything," Harlan murmurs. "We're here for you. No matter what." He squeezes my arm and walks away as I unfold the letter.

Dear Nova, it starts.

My throat tightens by the time I read the first sentence.

After the second paragraph, I'm shaking my head.

When I reach the third, my knees give out.

The staircase breaks my fall, my shoulder hitting the banister.

My eyes burn, making the lights blur together.

I force myself to read through to the end.

But even before I get there, I know the truth.

Clay isn't coming.

Not tonight.

Not ever.

He made his choice.

It's not me.

32

NOVA

One month later

November in Boston took a sharp cold turn, sending me scrambling for the winter clothes I hastily stuck in storage before my trip to Denver.

As I head home from the café, the wind blows inside the collar of my coat. I pull it tighter around me.

I text my new roommate a picture of me bundled up.

She responds almost immediately.

You still don't regret telling your old boss to fuck off?

Then, I'd have more salary for a car.

No, I reply.

It's true, most of the time.

The pay was better than at the café, though I get good tips some days.

I talked to Mari on the phone after she got back from her honeymoon, listening to her gush about the weather and the ocean and the food.

I've been ignoring social media. I don't have notifications turned on because I don't want to see anything Mari might be posting about the team, and ditto for Brooke or Chloe, whom I've followed since the wedding.

Except one night when I was out for a double date one of my old friends set me up on. We went to a sports bar, and the Kodiaks game was on. My date asked if I was into sports, and I said no.

"Wade's a beast, but he's overrated."

"No way, he'll come back this year," the other guy retorted. *"You seen the numbers he put up last week? He's a machine."*

"I heard he's a prick."

"He can be whatever he wants. Still gonna have the entire world lining up to suck his dick at the end of the night."

With every mention of the star player, my appetite faded away.

Clay didn't break my heart. He couldn't have, I reasoned, because we were never together.

But his letter is still buried in the back of my drawer.

It wasn't meant to be.

I'm not who you think.

We couldn't have been anything.

Clay's note passed through Harlan felt crueler than Brad's letter in the mailbox because I thought Clay and I understood one another. I hated that he wouldn't tell me to my face. I hated that he let me in, then slammed the door.

He made me feel stupid and gullible in a way I swore I wouldn't again.

On my way home from the double date, I searched his name.

Still nothing about a trade with LA, though there were low-level rumors the way there are about everything.

Why hasn't it worked out?

I shove down the question. His situation isn't my problem.

In between the news articles are images of him in his uniform, in press conferences. I came across one of him with a woman who looks a lot like the one who sent him naked pics in his car.

Damned Kodashians.

I like crunchy peanut butter.

Now you know something they don't.

Being angry is easier than being crushed.

So, I let myself be pissed for a few weeks in that hard, brittle way that covers up the fact that when it's late at night and I'm staring at the ceiling, I miss him more than I ever missed the man who offered to put a ring on my finger.

But each day, it's a little better.

I'm figuring things out. I'm moving on.

"You're her," a well-dressed woman says as I finish wiping down at the café.

"Excuse me?"

"I saw your art in a magazine. Your name was listed, and so I looked you up on social and saw that's who you were."

She pulls up her phone and shows me.

My drawing of Clay was featured in a magazine.

"You're very talented. I'd love to buy a piece."

I'm surprised and pleased. "I don't have any ready. Soon," I go on quickly.

I have been drawing lots since I got back to Boston. It's the one thing that's better, the only time I feel vibrant and alive.

She hands over a business card. "Call me when you do."

I've never sold a piece of my art, except for at the auction, which only half counts because people were supporting a charity. The prospect of earning money from my work is thrilling. I haven't let myself entertain that possibility since art school.

After promising I'll call her, I finish closing up at the café. I'm heading home from work as I go into my social media.

She's not the only one who found me.

As I walk up the stairs of the walkup, I see I'm tagged hundreds of times.

It's unbelievable.

But there's also an email.

Dear Nova,

I'm writing on behalf of the Kodiaks organization to invite you to create a special art installation to be completed on site in Denver.

Discretion is important, so if you intend to accept, please meet me to discuss the details and next steps.

Sincerely,

James Parker
Owner, Denver Kodiaks

What the hell?

It's mysterious and so hard to believe that I check the return email address to make sure it's not a hoax.

But it's the same format as Harlan's, only the name is different.

James Parker.

I thought I left this behind me.

Evidently not.

As kids, Mari and I used to set paper lanterns on fire every summer with our hopes and dreams in them. Seeing them float up into the darkness was freeing.

I stomp to my bedroom and dig through the back of my closet. My fingers close around Clay's jersey, and I yank it off the hanger it's been on since I put it there a month ago.

Back in the living room, I retrieve a lighter from the drawer in the coffee table.

This is moving forward. This is closure.

I huff out a breath as I hold the shirt up.

I flick the lighter until an orange flame dances on the end.

My heart accelerates.

Bad idea, Pink.

I shove the voice, his voice, down and lift the lighter to the corner of the jersey.

The fabric holds fast.

I grit my teeth.

Eventually a curl of smoke wafts up from the edge. The fabric darkens, beginning to blacken and melt.

A knock comes on my door.

Dammit.

Dropping the lighter and jersey on the couch, I cross the room and answer it.

Brooke is there wearing a full face of makeup and a Canada Goose parka.

"I thought you weren't coming until tomorrow?" I ask.

"Yeah, well, apparently, I came early to call an exterminator because your ass hasn't. I saw two rats *inside* the building," she insists, tugging her hood off.

I step back to let her in, and she throws her arms around me.

"It's good to see you," I murmur into her jacket, meaning it.

"Well, If I hadn't insisted on coming to visit my friend, it wouldn't have happened."

I take her coat and cross to the counter. "Wine?"

"Hell yes."

I pour two generous glasses and carry them back to the living area.

Brooke's perched on a chair like a queen holding court.

She lifts the jersey off the coffee table with her thumb and forefinger. "What the hell is this?"

I pass her a glass of wine and take a long gulp of mine. "Probably what it looks like."

My ass hits the couch, sending the lighter bouncing. My friend's eyes widen as she spots it.

"Were you going to burn this place down?!" she demands.

"I'm not crazy. I just wanted to be free."

"Smoking yourself out is not the answer." She shakes her head. "Whatever happened with you and Clay, you can't hide out here."

"Brooke, this is my life." I gesture around the apartment.

My friend stares me down. "You're too big for this."

"Square footage is less expensive than New York—"

"I mean your spirit, Nova. You were made for bigger things." She tosses the jersey at me, and I catch it, staring at the singed edge.

I think of the message that came in not long before she arrived.

"Since you mention it..." I set my wine down and reach for my phone, clicking into my email.

Brooke's eyes widen in glee as I pass it to her. "Oh my God. This is huge." She lets out a screech. "You have to say yes."

"There's no way. Why would Harlan make this offer?"

"I bet Harlan knows nothing about this. Rumor is he and James barely talk unless James is throwing his weight around."

This is making less sense by the second.

"He's crazy loaded, a 'no expenses spared' kind of guy," she goes on. "He made his money in finance and owns two jets and eight houses. If he's inviting you to do this, it isn't going to be any old installation. You have to say yes."

The mystery has me intrigued, I'll give her that.

"What if I don't want to go back?" I stare at the jersey, the half of Clay's name visible on the back.

"What if your future is waiting for you?" she counters.

"I already have a job."

"Yeah, because serving overpriced cappuccinos is your calling." She rolls her eyes, gesturing to the walls. "It's obvious you're not into art anymore."

My art is up all over the place. Every night, I've been drawing. It's compulsive. I can't stop.

I drain my glass and ball up the jersey in my fist, walking to the sink. I swear I feel his number burn itself into my skin as I set my glass down on the counter.

The email said the installation is at the venue.

Whatever LA deal Clay was trying to make hasn't gone through. If I take this job, there will be no avoiding him.

When I glance back, Brooke's typing on my phone.

"What are you doing?" I lunge for her.

She holds the phone away. "If you don't say yes, I will."

I snatch it back and stare at the email.

"Pack your bags," she says. "I can have a charter at Logan Airport in an hour."

I check my phone as I pace the room. "There's a home game tonight."

"We can steer clear of the stadium for now."

It's suddenly too warm in here. I lift the window over the sink, the cold air rushing in to burn my lungs.

"No." I square my shoulders. "I'm a big girl, and I'm over Clay. From here on out, this is about me."

Brooke's eyes flash with excitement. "Yes! This is going to be epic. I'll call for the plane."

"Wait! I have to do one thing first."

She turns back, questioning.

I take a breath before lifting the jersey.

"Pass me the lighter."

∼

Thank you for reading Game Changer! I hope you loved Clay and Nova's emotional, sexy romance.

Their story continues in Shot Taker, available to pre-order now at major bookstores.

xoxo,

Piper

He leads the league in scoring. My heart won't give him another shot.

I swore I'd never come back to Denver.
I'd never trust the wrong man again.
But here I am, back in the same place as the bad boy athlete who broke my heart.
Clay rules the basketball court, and now he's gunning for redemption. But I'm not the same girl who fell for the man behind the all-star image and reputation.
He made me want him like I've never wanted anyone.
He made me feel like I was the only thing that mattered.
A single look can make me ache.
A whispered promise in his gruff voice makes my chest tight.

Clay'll do anything to prove we're worth another shot.

Order Shot Taker now!

∽

For writing updates, early excerpts and exclusive giveaways...
Join my VIP List and never miss a thing!

∽

BOOKS BY PIPER LAWSON

FOR A FULL LIST PLEASE GO TO
PIPERLAWSONBOOKS.COM/BOOKS

OFF-LIMITS SERIES

Turns out the beautiful man from the club is my new professor... But he wasn't when he kissed me.

Off-Limits is a forbidden age gap college romance series. Find out what happens when the beautiful man from the club is Olivia's hot new professor.

WICKED SERIES

Rockstars don't chase college students. But Jax Jamieson never followed the rules.

Wicked is a new adult rock star series full of nerdy girls, hot rock stars, pet skunks, and ensemble casts you'll want to be friends with forever.

RIVALS SERIES

At seventeen, I offered Tyler Adams my home, my life, my heart. He stole them all.

Rivals is an angsty new adult series. Fans of forbidden romance, enemies to lovers, friends to lovers, and rock star romance will love these books.

ENEMIES SERIES

I sold my soul to a man I hate. Now, he owns me.

Enemies is an enthralling, explosive romance about an American DJ and a British billionaire. If you like wealthy, royal alpha males, enemies to lovers, travel or sexy romance, this series is for you!

TRAVESTY SERIES

My best friend's brother grew up. Hot.

Travesty is a steamy romance series following best friends who start a fashion label from NYC to LA. It contains best friends brother, second chances, enemies to lovers, opposites attract and friends to lovers stories. If you like sexy, sassy romances, you'll love this series.

PLAY SERIES

I know what I want. It's not Max Donovan. To hell with his money, his gaming empire, and his joystick.

Play is an addictive series of standalone romances with slow burn tension, delicious banter, office romance and unforgettable characters. If you like smart, quirky, steamy enemies-to-lovers, contemporary romance, you'll love Play.

ABOUT THE AUTHOR

Piper Lawson is a WSJ and USA Today bestselling author of smart and steamy romance.

She writes women who follow their dreams, best friends who know your dirty secrets and love you anyway, and complex heroes you'll fall hard for.

Piper lives in Canada with her tall and brilliant husband. She's a sucker for dark eyes, dark coffee, and dark chocolate.

For a complete reading list, visit
www.piperlawsonbooks.com/books

Subscribe to Piper's VIP email list
www.piperlawsonbooks.com/subscribe

- amazon.com/author/piperlawson
- bookbub.com/authors/piper-lawson
- instagram.com/piperlawsonbooks
- facebook.com/piperlawsonbooks
- goodreads.com/piperlawson

ACKNOWLEDGMENTS

Clay and Nova's story has taken me on a RIDE. I'm a huge basketball fan and have been desperate to write this story for years. I have loved going deeper into the lives of pro athletes and their teams, friends and families.

Game Changer wouldn't have happened without the support of my awesome readers, including my ARC team. You ladies provide endless enthusiasm, cheerleading, and help spreading the word.
Thank you.

Becca: Thank you for understanding me and my characters, and not giving up on us. Your wisdom and friendship brighten my world everyday.

Cassie: Thank you for being there when I need you. Your caring and consistency make it possible to do this wacky work year after year.

Devon: Thank you for making my words shine

without taking them from me. And for navigating the time difference. And for doing all this when you have better things to do.

Annette and Kate: Thank you for bringing the order and the fun, and knowing which days call for each. I don't know how I published a sentence without you. Don't ever leave me.

Lori and Emily: Thank you for taking an idea and making it a vibe. You're so talented and I'm grateful you still respond to my emails.

Monica: Thank you for bringing your beautiful brain and self to this book back when all the secondary characters were basically numbers.

Sara (and Mike): Thank you for the gorgeous images that have been living rent-free in my head the past two years, and for bringing Clay to life.

Nina and the VPR team: thank you for your advice, support, and for being good at talking to people when I'm not.

Last but not least, thank YOU for reading. Truly. Knowing we're living in these words and worlds together is the best part of any gig I've ever had.

Love always,

Piper

Printed in Great Britain
by Amazon